PRAISE FOR
THE BLOOD GUARD SERIES

"The humorous and exciting start of a new trilogy. . . .
The stakes are raised with a startling revelation that will have
readers eager for the next book."
—*Kirkus Reviews*

"Breathless action, witty dialogue, and unabashed fun."
—*Publishers Weekly*

"Wildly intense and deviously funny, *The Blood Guard* has real
heart as well as characters you'll fall in love with. This is cool stuff, very
cool stuff."
—Michael Grant, *New York Times* bestselling author of the Gone series

"A superbly written adventure. . . . Just the right amount of sar-
castic humor and genuine heart. . . . A great start to what is sure to be a
wildly popular series, especially among boys, and a must-have."
—*VOYA* (highlighted review)

"Intense, action-filled. . . . *The Blood Guard* is a non-put-downable
page-turner. . . . This book is a must-have."
—*The Guardian*

"*The Glass Gauntlet* is the exciting and long-awaited second book
in the Blood Guard series. . . . I can't wait to read what Carter Roy
will come up with next."
—*San Francisco Book Review*

"With strong character development, edge-of-your-seat pacing, and
fairly rich world building, *The Glass Gauntlet* is a strong sequel."
—*School Library Journal*

Also by Carter Roy

THE BLOOD GUARD
THE GLASS GAUNTLET

THE BLOOD GUARD

THE BLAZING BRIDGE

CARTER ROY

■SCHOLASTIC

Scholastic Children's Books
An imprint of Scholastic Ltd
Euston House, 24 Eversholt Street, London, NW1 1DB, UK
Registered office: Westfield Road, Southam, Warwickshire, CV47 0RA
SCHOLASTIC and associated logos are trademarks and/or
registered trademarks of Scholastic Inc.

First published in the UK by Scholastic Ltd, 2017

ISBN 978 1407 13701 8

A CIP catalogue record for this book
is available from the British Library.

Printed by CPI Group (UK) Ltd, Croydon, CR0 4YY
Papers used by Scholastic Children's Books are made
from wood grown in sustainable forests.

1 3 5 7 9 10 8 6 4 2

www.scholastic.co.uk

For Beth,
a hat trick;
and for Georgie,
the last line of the book

PROLOGUE
STOP ME IF YOU'VE HEARD THIS ONE BEFORE

Again and again this summer, I found myself climbing up the side of a burning building.

Okay, not *really*—this was a recurring dream, my brain rerunning a real-life nightmare from months earlier. (Thanks a lot, brain.)

It always starts like this:

Smoke swirls around me, but so do flurries of snow. My hands, chest, and toes are practically broiling against a wall of scorching-hot brick. That's when I remember: I'm stuck on the front of our burning brownstone in the middle of a snowstorm.

When I look up, the edge of the roof is impossibly far away. I know I'll never reach it. So I look down instead.

Bad move.

I am so dizzyingly high that the cars parked on the

street look like Hot Wheels, and the snowy yard in front of our brownstone seems about as big as a postage stamp. Everything is lit up a creepy carnival orange thanks to the crackling flames.

Fear wallops me. My breath sticks in my throat, my fingers cramp, my right foot slips, and—

I hug the wall and catch myself.

Then, because I have no choice, I keep going up.

I climb for what feels like hours.

And here's the amazing thing: I make it. My groping hand feels only air because I've reached the top.

And then someone grabs my arm.

It's my dad. He's clean shaven and wearing a pin-striped suit, like he's just stopped by on his way to an important meeting—never mind the snow, ash, and smoke.

He's got hold of me, so I raise my other hand to pull myself over.

That's when he says, "My work here is done, Evelyn."

It sounds like a punch line, but he isn't the kind of dad who jokes around.

Then he lets go.

And just like that, I'm falling to my death.

He watches. I can see his face over the edge of the roof, the front of the building an inferno, and we lock eyes until, with a full-body flinch, I jolt awake.

In real life, Dad hadn't been waiting on the roof, but he *was* the one who'd burned our house down. I'd heard lots of explanations for why he'd done it, but none of them ever made any sense.

That dream nagged at me all summer, but I kept it to myself. I didn't want Dawkins or my mom to think I wasn't ready to join the Blood Guard. I wanted to solve the puzzle of this dream on my own.

You're missing something, you idiot, I kept telling myself.

But what?

CHAPTER 1
A DARK AND STORMY FLIGHT

My dream was true about one important thing: Heights? They utterly terrify me now.

Most of the time, the fear wasn't a big deal. How many times in everyday life do you find yourself staring down at your certain death? Not all that often.

So I hardly felt nervous at all during the helicopter flight from Agatha Glass' estate. I was sitting between my friends Sammy and Greta on the leather-covered back bench, a helmet on my head, the four Dobermans of the apocalypse curled up warm against my feet, and it was easy to forget that we were zooming through the twilight sky in a noisy little glass bubble, thousands of feet above the ground.

We had taken the copter and left the rest of the Blood Guard behind. It was the fastest way to get to Greta's house in Brooklyn and convince her mom to come into hiding before my father and his evil flunkies showed up.

My dad is a bigwig in a murderous organization called the Bend Sinister. They're working to bring about the end of the world by finding and killing thirty-six special "Pure" souls who keep the world in balance. The Pure at the top of his hit list just happens to be my best friend, Greta.

Greta doesn't *know* she's a Pure . . . and I can't tell her. It was one of the very first lessons Dawkins taught me: self-knowledge *changes* a Pure, deep down. If Greta found out the truth, she would lose the very quality that makes her so special, the quality that makes her a Pure. And then the world would begin to end.

But my dad had learned the truth about Greta. And since he couldn't get to her, we guessed he would go after Greta's mom.

So we had to get to her first.

We had almost reached New York—flying over some little town in northern New Jersey—when Agatha threw us into a steep dive. The world through the helicopter's canopy tilted, and a bunch of blocky buildings like models in an old train set rushed at us.

"Flying under the radar to keep our approach to New York a secret," she explained. "You can never be too safe."

"Ahhh!" I yelped, and tried not to hyperventilate. "Why's everything dark?"

"Because you covered your eyes," Greta said, prying

my hands down, her face invisible in her giant flight helmet. "Gross. You're all sweaty."

"Because we're so high up," I said, staring straight at the back of Agatha's and Dawkins' seats.

"You're afraid of heights?" Greta asked.

"Didn't you tell me some crazy story about how you climbed the front of a burning house?" Sammy asked, skeptical.

"That was *different*," I mumbled, rubbing at the scar across my palm. "This is . . ."

We leveled out a hundred feet or so, soaring through the early night sky. On the floor facing me, Agatha's four Dobermans blinked and tilted their heads. Their bulbous headphones made them look especially judgmental.

"Stop looking at me like that," I told them. "I am *not* going to be sick."

"They don't believe you, Ronan," Dawkins said, cranking his body around. He handed me a white paper airsickness bag. "And neither do I." Jack Dawkins is like your best friend's annoying older brother—a skinny hipster who acts all worldly even though he looks like he's still in his teens. Thing is, with Dawkins, he *is* all worldly, on account of being almost two centuries old. "This new fear of heights may be an after-effect of that near-death escape Sammy mentioned. Traumatic experiences leave thumbprints on the emotions, you know."

7

"But this is all new," I said. "I used to be fine."

"Perhaps your psyche has finally snapped . . . like an overloaded graham cracker." He licked his lips. "Anyone else wishing we'd eaten dinner before departing?" Dawkins is always, *always* hungry.

"My psyche is *not* like a graham cracker," I insisted.

"Whatever the case, this fear of yours may well disappear if you simply tackle it head-on," Dawkins ended.

"Maybe," I said.

The copter bounced up and down.

"Bit of turbulence—sorry!" Agatha called back. Like Dawkins, she's old but looks super young—a two-hundred-year-old woman magically trapped in a nine-year-old's body. She had to use a booster seat in the pilot's chair, which didn't help me feel a whole lot safer, to be perfectly honest. "We'll be back down before you know it!"

"That's what I'm afraid of," I muttered.

"Easy, Ronan," Greta whispered, wiping my face with the sleeve of her green hoodie.

"I'll be okay." I made myself grin. It wasn't easy. "Crazy to think that we'll be home in like twenty minutes!"

"*Crazy* is right." Greta's smile faltered. "How am I going to explain all of this to my mom?"

Good question. Somehow Greta was going to have to convince her mom that Greta's dad had had a secret identity for most of the time they'd been married. Mr.

Sustermann was, like my mom, a member of the Blood Guard, the ancient order of sword-swinging, butt-kicking knights who protect the thirty-six Pure from those who would do them harm.

Would Mrs. Sustermann even believe her? I may not have believed my mom, if I hadn't witnessed her leap thirty feet through the air and use a sword to deflect bullets. That sort of thing will make a believer out of anybody.

"Yeah, it's going to be *very* weird," I agreed. "Still, it'll be nice to be home."

"You don't even have a home anymore," Greta said, frowning. "It's just an empty lot now."

Some part of me understood, of course, that our blackened, burnt-out house wouldn't still be standing. But *knowing* a thing and *feeling* it aren't the same, and for a moment, my stomach clenched. My old life really *was* long gone.

Back when I lived on First Place a year and a half ago, I was just a stressed-out, over-scheduled middle schooler with a distracted dad and a way-too-intense mom—basically, just like any other kid in our Brooklyn neighborhood. All of that went up in flames when my father put our home to the torch.

I gasped.

"What is it now?" Greta asked.

"It's just . . ." I pointed. "That."

We were flying over water now, the glimmering

skyscrapers of New York City rising from the darkness ahead of us.

"Wow," Sammy said, leaning forward. "Unreal!"

Even I had to admit: it *did* look pretty glorious. The shadowy towers were speckled with lights, and the streets below glowed gold from all the cars and streetlamps. I'd missed the city. I'd forgotten how beautiful it is.

There was no place for Agatha to land in Brooklyn, so the plan was to touch down at a helipad in lower Manhattan where Dawkins had arranged for another Blood Guard to meet us. That person would drive us to Greta's house "with all haste and lead-footed abandon," according to Dawkins.

Raindrops suddenly drummed against the canopy, and the four Dobermans began growling.

"It's just a little rain," Dawkins said, scratching one of the dogs' heads.

War, Famine, Pestilence, and Debra strained at their safety harnesses.

"Maybe they're disappointed that the Statue of Liberty is so small," Sammy said. Out the left-hand window was the familiar greenish-white monument.

"It's a lot bigger up close," Greta said. "And on this side is the Brooklyn Bridge."

Sammy turned. "Why is it so orange?"

I risked a glance. It was true: a third of the bridge was bright orange, like it had been wrapped in an enormous tent. "That *is* weird," I said. The view blurred as rain hammered against the glass.

Agatha strained against the joystick as the copter bucked and then dropped thirty feet.

Greta held her stomach. "This is making even *me* feel sick."

"A good thing we're so close." Agatha wrestled the controls as the copter rocked from side to side. "The heliport is right off the West Side Highway."

"Maybe if you take us lower, we can escape the worst of it," Dawkins said.

But closer to the churning black waters of the Hudson, the rain didn't let up. If anything, it got heavier.

And then the inside of the cabin pulsed with blinding light.

"Lightning?" Agatha said as a second bolt of electricity sizzled through the air.

I blinked away a soft violet afterimage.

"That was close!" Greta said.

"*Too* close," Dawkins said. "Worse, it was going the wrong direction."

"Wrong direction?" Agatha repeated, bringing us still lower.

"Usually lightning goes from the *clouds* to the *ground*. Those bolts are coming from directly in front of us."

"The Bend Sinister," Greta said.

"We have a welcoming party," Dawkins said.

"Though how they knew we were coming, I can't say."
His eyes flicked to Agatha.

"*I* didn't tell anyone," she protested. "I've been with
you the whole time!"

"I trust you," he said. "It's the circumstances I mis-
trust. Is this your usual flight path?"

"It is," she said. I wouldn't have thought such a
little kid could slump into herself, but Agatha seemed to
shrink behind the pilot's seat. "And if anyone had been
watching, they would have seen us lift off."

"Right," Dawkins said. "And someone might have
been watching thanks to Ronan's dad. We're going to
come in hot, everybody."

"They probably made this storm, too," I said,
remembering how a Bend Sinister Hand and one of her
agents had made a river flow backward. If they could
do *that*, then creating a thunderstorm shouldn't be too
tricky. "Some of them can control nature."

"True—when enough of them work together. We'll
be lucky if it's only five agents and a Hand. Any more
than that and we'll likely end up in the drink." Dawkins
flipped some switches on the dash. "Would you mind,
Agatha, if I take the controls?"

"Flying's not as easy as it looks," Agatha replied.

"I piloted a Huey a half century ago in Vietnam;
trust me, I can handle this little bird." A burst of violet
light shot forth from the dark line of the shore ahead,
and Dawkins flicked the helicopter left. The Tesla bolt

crackled past just over the rotors, leaving a lavender shadow on my eyelids.

"The helicopter's rotor blades," I stammered. "Would that spell you use on swords work on something that big?" I'd seen it used only twice—once when my mom enchanted a sword before facing two Bend Sinister agents who were armed with pistols, and another time when Dawkins used it on a pocketknife.

Dawkins laughed. "A fine idea!" Then he whispered a quick, pretty singsong in some other language, weaving the fingers of his left hand in the air. As he finished, a new light shone down upon us: a pale blue glow radiating from the rotors overhead. "Now we have a shield!" Dawkins said. "But alas, only one way to use it—we have to come in at an angle. Forgive me, Ronan."

"For wha—?" I started to say, and then he tipped the copter forward so sharply that all of us dangled in our harnesses—even the dogs. Their claws scrabbled against the metal bulkhead.

Now all I could see through the helicopter's canopy was the frothing dark water of the river. We were flying at a forty-five degree angle, using the glowing rotors to shield the cabin.

"Now I think *I'm* going to be sick," Sammy said, pinwheeling his arms in the air.

By raising my head I could just make out a concrete strip of land in front of us. Five silhouettes were lined up across it. They were haloed by a bunch of small white lights—the helipad landing guide. Just beyond them was the West Side Highway, buzzing with nighttime traffic.

"You're heading straight for them!" I said.

"*We* have the deadlier weapon, Ronan—let's see how they handle *this*." A Tesla bolt struck the rotors dead-on and was deflected, lavender crackles of light arcing away on all sides.

"You're going to crash!" Agatha shouted.

"No, I am not," Dawkins replied. "Trust me."

"Hold tight!" Dawkins goosed the throttle, and the copter surged forward, rotors-first.

All four Dobermans began howling.

Greta and Sammy shrieked with what sounded like their last breaths.

I would have joined them, but I was too busy throwing up.

CHAPTER 2
THE BIZ WITH DIZ

I didn't see what happened next: I was too busy filling the paper sack Dawkins had given to me. But I heard and felt everything.

At the last moment, Dawkins must have yanked on the joystick so that the copter—and its deadly spinning blades—tilted back. In a split second, we went from dangling forward in our harnesses to slamming against the rear bulkhead. Through the front window, I glimpsed the brand-new Freedom Tower.

The engine coughed once, then conked out.

We fell.

And then we crashed.

The impact shook us all—the bruises from my harness were going to last for weeks—but what really shocked me was how loud it was. Dropping three tons of metal and glass onto a concrete helipad from fifty feet in the air makes a lot of noise. All the windows shattered, the supports for one of the skids thrust up through the dash just inches from Agatha, and the cabin walls crunched inward like the sides of an accordion.

Warm rain blew into the cabin through the smashed canopy.

One of the dogs whined in the sudden silence.

And then Agatha cried, "You ruined my helicopter!"

"Sorry," Dawkins said. "I'd tell you I'll pay you for it, but we both know I haven't got the scratch."

Greta shrugged off her helmet. "Why are we so crooked?"

"Two of the Bend Sinister agents softened our landing," Dawkins said, slipping between the pilot seats. He released the dogs and wrenched open the left-hand door. The cabin rocked back and forth. "And clearly they're not quite out for the count." Stooping, Dawkins withdrew a cutlass from a duffel bag on the floor. "See that bunker yonder?" Back toward the water was a cinder block building as big as a two-car garage. "Leg it over there. The dogs and I will take care of our welcoming party." The steel came clear of its scabbard with a crisp metallic hum.

"After me," Agatha said. She leaped down out of the open door, Greta and Sammy right behind her.

I was about to join them when Dawkins handed me a sword. "Drop that sack and take this."

I looked at my hand—I was still holding the

airsickness bag. I threw it to the floor, grabbed the weapon, and climbed down to the tarmac.

Within moments, we were all soaked to our skin.

"Enough gadding about," Dawkins said, pointing with his blade. "*Run!*"

Greta, Sammy, and Agatha splashed away into the dark, but Dawkins' hand held me back. "Not you, Ronan. I need you here."

Sure, I'd just puked out my guts, survived a helicopter crash, and was now so wet that I could feel water squishing in my socks, but suddenly none of that mattered.

"What's the plan?" I asked.

"We've squashed two agents, but three or four are still out there. I'll draw their attention so the dogs can do their thing, and then, once everyone is busy, see if you can't sneak around and take out the closest agent." He whistled low, and then he and the dogs flowed around the front of the cabin and out of sight.

I went the other way, edging around the rear of the helicopter until I could see three agents through the rain. One woman with long black hair held a Tesla rifle in her arms. Another woman, a redhead, was armed with a saber. The third figure, a bald guy, had his head thrown back and was slowly moving his hands in the air like he was conducting a symphony—directing the rainstorm, I guessed.

"Why don't you two put down your weapons,"

Dawkins said, walking toward them, "and no one else will have to get hurt."

The woman with the black hair growled and leveled her gun.

"Was afraid that'd be your response," Dawkins said, dropping into a squat as she fired.

He disappeared.

I didn't know he could do that! I'd seen my mom make huge leaps while she was running, but vanishing into thin air?

The Tesla bolt crackled across the empty space where Dawkins had been, rain sizzling off the beam. Then the woman swung the muzzle of her gun in my direction.

She'd seen me.

That was when Dawkins hurtled down from the sky, his knees tucked to his chest like a kid cannonballing into a swimming pool—right onto the bald man who was conducting the storm.

Dawkins had *jumped*, I realized—straight up into the rainy dark.

The impact of Dawkins' body knocked the man unconscious. And just like that, the storm stopped, like someone had flipped a switch.

Dawkins sprang to his feet, cutlass raised, in time to block the blow of the swordswoman.

The black-haired woman with the rifle glanced at them but didn't seem in a hurry to help. She smiled and turned back to aiming her gun. At me.

I can't jump like Dawkins—I'm not even a Blood Guard yet, and I don't have the skills he and my mom do. I threw myself to the ground and covered my head with my hands.

The shot never came.

Instead, there was an explosion of furious growling and angry shrieks.

The dogs.

Four black-and-tan shadows swarmed over the woman, pulling her down, nipping at her arms and legs. They looked like they were wrestling. Every time the agent managed to work an arm or leg free from one dog's jaws, another dog lunged across her and caught the limb between its teeth. She never stopped bucking and thrashing and fighting them, not even after they dragged her into the heavy shadows at the edge of the landing pad.

The woman's shouts covered the sound of my sword coming free of its scabbard. Crouching low, I went to help Dawkins.

He and the swordswoman hadn't paused in their duel. She grinned crazily the whole time.

"You'll never escape," the woman said, gleeful. "I've alerted everyone to your arrival! The Bend Sinister are all over New York City."

"Oh, *please*," Dawkins said. With a flurry of swift attacks, he drove her back toward the copter. And me. "That's a lie. You don't have near enough people to cover

19

the city."

"The truth," she said, lowering her weapon. "*Hundreds* of teams. More than enough to overwhelm one Blood Guard Overseer and a handful of children."

I was nearly within range. I lifted the point of my weapon, readying my attack.

Dawkins lunged.

With a laugh, the redheaded woman dodged him. She swung around and slammed the hilt of her blade against his head as he stumbled past.

He sprawled face-first on the ground, stunned, his sword spinning away across the wet pavement.

"And I will take care of those kids as easily as I have taken care of you." Standing over him, the woman clasped her sword between both hands and raised it overhead. She glanced over her shoulder at me and winked. "You're next, little boy."

There was no way I could close the thirty feet between us in time, no way to stop her from sticking her blade through Dawkins' back.

But I had to do *something*.

So I shouted "No!" and ran at her.

Before I'd gone even six steps, the piercing shriek of a car horn stopped me dead. With a shrill scrape of metal, a boxy little yellow cab leaped the curb. It was the jazziest cab I'd ever seen, with glowing flat screens on the sides and hood and across the top like a high-tech dorsal fin.

And it was totally out of control.

The cab whirled around on the rain-slicked concrete—once, twice, its tires squealing, water fanning behind it, momentum carrying it past twenty feet to my right. But the third time it spun, the car abruptly stopped. Still poised with her blade raised above her head, the swordswoman was caught dead center in the headlights.

Then the cab roared straight at her.

The swordswoman jumped back, but the driver was ready for that. As the cab shot between the Bend Sinister agent and Dawkins, the cabbie kicked open his door and knocked the swordswoman right off her feet. She bounced against the fender and fell to the ground.

"What happened?" Dawkins asked, getting to his knees.

"An insane cab driver," I said, giving him a hand.

At the far end of the heliport, the cab did the bootlegger maneuver my mom had shown me back at the start of the summer—using the emergency brake to swing the back end of the car around 180 degrees. And then slowly rolled back our way.

As the taxi pulled up, Dawkins wrenched down the jacket of the unconscious swordswoman and did some complicated knotting of the sleeves so that the woman's arms were pinned. "Our ride. Just in the nick of time."

"That crazy cabbie—*he's* our ride?" I asked.

"*She*," said the cabbie, opening her door. She was

tall, and made even taller by her piles of upswept pink hair. "And I'd be a little more complimentary, considering this 'crazy cabbie' just saved your life." She tugged down her dress, adjusted a chunky silver necklace, and pulled an umbrella from her cab. Like her dress, it was patterned with big flowers. I couldn't be sure, because of her dark cat's-eye shades, but she seemed to be sizing me up. Apparently satisfied, she flipped up the lenses of her sunglasses. "You're okay," she said. "But you should stop staring. Might make a girl self-conscious."

"Um, sure," I said. "I mean, I was just looking at your hair."

Her red lips parted into a smile. "Do you like it? It's called a beehive." She pointed at the unconscious bald man. "That's one, and the woman is two. Where are the others?"

"Two are under that crashed helicopter—"

"Let me guess," said the cabbie, tilting her head and squinting at Dawkins. "*You* were the pilot?"

"Yes, but I took out *two* of them, so it was a *strategic* crash." Dawkins put his fingers to his mouth and whistled. "There was a fifth agent, with a gun, but the dogs carried her off."

The Dobermans trotted toward us, towing the female agent across the pavement, each latched on to a wrist or pant leg or, in the case of Pestilence, a muzzle's worth of suit coat. We met them halfway, the cabbie stooping to bind the woman's hands with thin plastic strips from her car. "Zip ties," she said when she saw me staring. "It's what the police use instead of handcuffs nowadays."

Dawkins leaned over to scratch the dogs' ears, their wagging tails thumping his legs. "Good work, my fearsome four!"

"This woman makes five," said the cabbie as she stood up again. "But where's their Hand?" She flipped her shades back down and turned a slow circle. As she did I saw something I hadn't noticed before: one lens was thicker than the other.

I walked up close to get a better look. "Is that a Verity Glass?" I whispered. "Built into your sunglasses?"

"Works almost like night-vision goggles," she quietly replied. Then to Dawkins, she said, "I don't see any other Bend Sinister nearby."

"Oh, but you will soon enough!" cried our captive. The rain had slicked her long dark hair across her face so that I couldn't see her eyes, but the crazy menace in her voice was clear enough. "I am legion, and I will come for you!"

"*You're* a pleasant one," Dawkins said as Greta, Sammy, and Agatha ran up, breathless.

"You two okay?" Greta asked.

Sammy said, "We saw that jump, Jack—you shot like fifty feet into the air!"

Just then, a black sedan pulled up along the curb

on the West Side Highway. A man in a cap climbed out and waved.

Agatha waved back. "My driver. Since everything here's under control, I'll make good my escape and—"

"You will never escape!" The Bend Sinister agent couldn't see us through the wet blanket of her hair, but she clearly had no trouble hearing. Or talking. "I told that lousy swordsman, the Bend Sinister will soon be here in force."

"Then we should get moving, too, Jack," said the cabbie.

"Just a moment," Dawkins replied, crouching and pulling the woman's hair away from her face. She snapped her teeth at his fingers. "First," he said, "I am an *excellent* swordsman. Second, it wasn't *you* I fought, so how do you know what that agent said to me? Are *you* the Hand?"

"Yes! No!" said the woman, thrashing on the ground. "I am and am not who you are looking for." She craned her head around until she could see the helicopter. "Why don't you ask *them*."

From beneath the helicopter, the trapped agents gurgled out insults. "I am legion!"

"I'm here! I'm there! I'm everywhere!"

"This is pointless, Jack," said the cabbie. "You heard her—other agents are on their way. These games of hers are a delaying tactic."

But Dawkins had one last question. "Was it Head

Truelove who warned you we were coming?"

I flinched. Yes, my dad is a bad guy and his name is my name, too. Some things you just never get over.

"Truelove?" The agent broke into high-pitched witchy laughter. "That cowardly failure? That shameful outcast? That witless charlatan? That—"

"We get it," Dawkins said. "You don't like him."

"Truelove is out! He's done! He's washed up! He's good as dead!"

"That's enough." Dawkins stood. "Okay, everyone— we're going now."

"Tell me about the cabbie," Agatha said, nodding at the taxi. The driver, her umbrella tucked under an arm, was looking at her reflection in her windshield and reapplying her lipstick.

"Her real name is Darlene, but the last person to call her that . . ." Dawkins shivered. "She goes by Diz."

Agatha smiled. "See you again at the meet-up." And then she jogged toward the waiting car.

"Meter's ticking, kids!" Diz popped her lipstick into a tiny pink clutch. "It's time to run."

From behind her, the bald man roused, sat up, and announced, "Run run run, just as fast as you can!" He laughed—raspier and deeper than the black-haired woman, but somehow sounding exactly the same.

"Quiet, you," said Diz, twirling her umbrella. The brass handle caught the man's head with a loud *crack* and he slumped down again.

"The Hand can't be *all* these Bend Sinister agents," Dawkins said as he climbed into the front passenger seat. "And yet they all speak like a Hand."

"Strap in, everyone," Diz said, watching us in the rearview mirror.

Greta, Sammy, and I clicked our seat belts into place just as Diz stabbed the gas. The car gunned across the tarmac toward the highway. At the last moment, she hooked the wheel hard right.

Tires shrieking, the back end swung around behind us as the cab slid sideways, right into an open slot between two speeding cars. And just like that, we were part of the flow of traffic heading south.

"Nice maneuver," Greta said.

"Thanks!" Diz studied Greta in the rearview mirror. I wondered how Diz could even stay on the road while staring at the brilliance of a Pure through her Verity Glass. Whenever I looked at Greta through mine, I was practically blinded.

Which reminded me of someone. "Maybe this Hand is like Patch Steiner," I said to Dawkins. Beside me, Sammy and Greta tensed at the mention of the enormous blind Hand we'd run into only days before, who was able to steal the senses—vision, hearing, balance, and more—of anyone he chose. I wasn't thrilled at the idea of having to face another Patch Steiner. One had been bad enough. "Except instead of swiping a person's eyesight or whatever, he takes over their entire bodies."

"But can this mysterious Hand possess just *any* soft-brained yahoo?" Dawkins wondered. "Or only Bend Sinister agents?"

"He didn't take over any of *us*, did he?" Diz pointed out. "He only switched between the five agents back there."

"Hmm, good point," Dawkins said. And then he reached toward three silver buttons set in a row where most cars would have a radio. "What are all these shiny new things?"

Diz slapped his hand away. "Don't touch! It's no picnic being a woman cab driver in a nasty old city like New York. So I've added some protective measures to my ride." She grinned, and I saw a bit of dark red lipstick on her front teeth.

"Ejector seats?" Dawkins said, clasping his hands together. "Flamethrowers? Please tell me there are flamethrowers."

"Oh, stop," Diz said. "Nothing so ridiculous."

"Is that why you have a Verity Glass built into your sunglasses?" I asked.

She tapped her glasses. "No, this is so I can monitor the movements of the Bend Sinister."

The Verity Glass didn't just reveal the radiance of a Pure soul, I knew from experience. It also unmasked agents of the Bend Sinister. Through the Glass, they appeared as outlines, shimmery shadows of real people. They'd given up that deep *something* that made them human, and the Glass showed that they walked the world as mere husks of who they'd been before.

"Have new teams of agents shown up in the city?" Dawkins asked.

"Tons," Diz said. "It's *bad*, Jack. Their numbers started increasing late last spring, and now they're everywhere, blending in with regular folks—businesspeople and police officers and students and the homeless—you name it."

"So that Hand wasn't lying." Dawkins drummed his fingers on the dash. "He said there were more than a hundred teams here."

"But why? What are they doing here?" Sammy wondered.

Greta clutched the back of Dawkins' seat. "Is this because of us? Are they here to stop us from rescuing my mom?"

"Not if they started showing up last spring." Dawkins shook his head. "No, this is about something else, something bigger."

Late last spring. That was when the Bend Sinister captured a Pure named Flavia. And also when my dad finally blew his cover and took off. I said as much. "But what does all of that have to do with this?"

"I haven't the foggiest idea," Dawkins replied. "And that is what terrifies me."

CHAPTER 3

HOME IS WHERE
THE HURT IS

Sammy was the first to notice the change in the light. "What's going on?" he asked.

The inside of the car had filled with a soft orange glow, and when we looked out the window, the night was gone and the sky had turned tangerine.

"It's that artist," Diz said, waving her hand at the world outside the windshield. "Krisco. He's wrapping up the Brooklyn Bridge in silk."

"But *why* is this Krisco guy covering up the bridge?" I asked. The silk stretched in solid, carrot-colored panels from below the roadway all the way up to the suspension cables. Even the stone support towers had been wrapped up. The only uncovered thing was the three-lane roadway. I couldn't see the city, the East River, or the traffic going the other way—just orange and more orange everywhere I looked.

"Does there have to be a reason?" Diz asked. "I think it looks kind of cool."

"What about the Manhattan side?" I asked. "That half of the bridge was normal. Isn't that part of the art project?"

"The artwork isn't finished yet," Diz said. "I guess it takes a long time to wrap up an entire bridge."

"And a lot of silk," I said.

"How is wrapping something up *art*?" Sammy asked.

Normally, this was the sort of question that would unlock the know-it-all nerd within Greta and get her talking, but her mind must have been on her mom. She didn't even acknowledge Sammy's question, just quietly stared out the window.

Sammy shook his head. "I mean, *I* could wrap up things—and do a better job. Look at that raggedy stuff dangling down behind us!"

I looked back. Along the unfinished edge of the project, loose panels of silk fluttered in the wind.

Art or not, I was glad to be on the Brooklyn Bridge. Even wrapped in pumpkin-colored silk, it was unmistakable. It looked like the gateway to my old neighborhood, like a giant signpost the world had put up to let me know that I was coming home at last.

Dawkins had been quiet the whole time we were crossing the bridge. Now, as we came off the end of it, he muttered, "We've overlooked something."

"The artwork?" I asked, looking back over my shoulder. "Is there more to it?"

"No, no—forget the orange silk; that's not important. I want to solve this puzzle. What are so many of the Bend Sinister doing here? First, we need to identify the pieces. Ronan, you'll recall that Ms. Hand and her team were only one of several pursuing you and your mother last spring."

"That's true," I said, remembering that strange day in Stanhope when my mother picked me up from school and forever changed my life. "There were probably three or four groups after us."

"Far more than necessary to capture a thirteen-year-old boy. But not if the Bend Sinister were already in the area. So that's one piece of the puzzle: they were here for some other reason."

"And Ms. Hand was hauling weapons," Greta said, suddenly snapping back to attention. "Lots of guns, with Tesla modifications." During our escape, Greta and I had dumped a crate full of their weapons into a river.

"That's the second piece," Dawkins said, raising two fingers. "They were bringing armaments to someone. Probably in this very city. For what purpose?"

Diz turned the cab down my old street. We passed the space where my family's brownstone used to be, but there was nothing to see—just shadow and a patch of stars between the buildings on either side.

"And then Truelove"—Dawkins glanced back at me—"sorry, Ronan. And then Truelove actually brought the Pure soul he'd captured to Agatha Glass' estate. Why? That's hardly a sensible thing to do with such a valuable prize. We'll call that action the third puzzle piece."

I thought about my recurring nightmare. Was that one of the puzzle pieces, too?

Greta sighed. "And what about how the Bend Sinister *knew* we were coming—they were *waiting* at the heliport. So they must know we're going to my mom's house."

Dawkins faced her. "Greta, that would be my conclusion, too, but there's one thing those agents said that gives me hope."

"The stuff about my dad," I said.

"Precisely. It sounds as though Mr. Truelove is on the outs with his old cronies."

"Which could mean," I finished, "that the Bend Sinister don't know that Greta is helping the Blood Guard, and they might not be going after her mom."

"I think it's time I call her," Greta said. "You said once we got close, and we're almost there."

"After that welcoming party at the heliport, we can't risk it. If the Bend Sinister are laying a trap, then they will have tapped her phone." Dawkins said. "For safety's sake, it is best we just show up and spirit her away."

"This is my *mom*, Jack," Greta said, her voice gravelly. "She's not like Ronan's mom, and she's not like my dad. She's just a regular person."

Dawkins reached back and rested a hand on Greta's shoulder. "Nothing bad will happen to her, Greta. I give you my word." He faced forward again and whispered to Diz, "*Hurry*."

Diz turned down the street before Greta's, scanning the sidewalks with her modified sunglasses, making sure no agents were lurking in the neighborhood. We rolled past a pair of familiar half-white, half-green globe lampposts—a staircase into the subway.

After circling around for a good five minutes, Diz finally took us down Greta's old street. "There's not a soul out that I can see," Diz said. She stopped the cab alongside a line of parked cars. "We're sitting ducks, double-parked like this in front of the house, so make it snappy. I'll cover you from the street."

"Here we are, Greta," Dawkins said. "Home sweet home."

I looked out at Greta's house. She and I hadn't been friends when I lived in Brooklyn, but a kid I knew from the ILZ gamer boards lived near the corner, and I'd walk past Greta's on the way to his place. The Sustermanns lived in a brownstone, like the one my family had, but theirs just looked *happier* somehow. Her mom or dad had built a lush little garden in the front yard, with a bench and a fountain in the corner, and there were flowerboxes on the windowsills, and all sorts of little touches that said home. Like the white light glowing over the porch now.

As I stared at it, the light blinked off, plunging the front of the house into darkness.

"That was . . . unexpected," Dawkins said, wrapping his right hand around the hilt of his sword.

"Very." Diz studied the house and yard. "But I don't see anything amiss. Maybe she's going to bed early?"

"What do you think, Greta?" Dawkins turned in his seat, that crazy smile of his on his face. "Is your mum the sort to turn in at nine—hey now, what's that for?"

None of us had noticed that Greta had silently been crying. Diz handed back a fistful of tissues, and Greta wiped her face and blew her nose. "I'm not *sad*," she said. "Really. I'm just . . . I really missed my mom." She hiccupped a laugh. "I sort of didn't believe I'd ever see her again."

"Well, you won't if you just sit here bawling," Dawkins said, opening his door. "Pull yourself together. It's time for your homecoming."

Greta's house wasn't all that nice anymore.

It almost looked like no one lived there. In the dim light of the streetlamp, I could see that the plants were all dry and dead looking. The fountain was still noisily burbling, but even it looked pretty gross—mossy and green and overflowing because the basin was clogged or something.

Greta frowned. "It's not like my mom to let her plants die. Unless she was really depressed."

"Maybe she had a busy summer," Dawkins replied quietly. "Me, I've never been able to keep a plant alive for longer than an hour or two."

We followed Greta from the gate along a stone path, past the basement stairs, and silently climbed the flight of steps that led up to the now-dark front door.

Sammy and I waited to one side behind Dawkins, while Greta stretched her finger toward the doorbell button. "Feels weird to ring the bell at my own house."

"You don't have a key?" Sammy asked.

"Sure," Greta said. "I mean, I did, but I left it back in Wilson Peak along with the rest of my stuff."

"Probably buried in ash and burnt trees," Sammy said.

"Probably," Greta agreed.

"Bummer," I said. Even though I'd hated spending my summer in the ghost town of Wilson Peak, training with Sammy and Greta to join the Blood Guard, I still felt a pang thinking about how the Bend Sinister had burned the place to the ground.

I listened to the water splash in the fountain below us, wary all of a sudden. It had been stupid for all of us to come up the stairs; Sammy and I should have stayed in the cab with Diz. And I should have brought

35

a weapon, too. Up on these stone steps, ten feet above the ground, we could be trapped.

Greta pressed the bell. A pleasant chiming came from inside. But no lights turned on, and no one came to the door.

"Let me have a look." Dawkins gently pushed Greta aside, pressed his face against the glass of the door, and peered inside. "I don't see any sign of your mum or of struggle. Still, you can never be too safe." He drew his sword.

We were all watching Dawkins—which is why none of us noticed the person behind us until it was too late.

A figure in a black hoodie rushed up the stairs, shoved Dawkins against the door, rammed the muzzle of a pistol into the back of his skull, and growled, "Drop the sword or I'll *kill* you."

"*Mom?*" Greta said. "Mom, it's *me*! These are my friends!"

The figure stepped back, still pointing the gun at Dawkins, and with her other hand pulled back her hood. Underneath was a face I knew: Greta's mother, but somehow looking a lot different than the last time I'd seen her. The long blond hair was gone; it was jaw length now, and she'd lost a lot of weight. She'd always been about the same height as her daughter, but now she was skinny like her, too—on the dark porch, they almost looked like sisters.

"Greta?" she whispered, staring at her. She cast

quick glances at me, Sammy, and Dawkins, and the unsheathed sword in his hand. "You're supposed to be in witness protection. What are you doing here?"

But that was all she managed to get out before Greta crushed her in a fierce hug.

Her mom hugged her right back while the rest of us just stood there awkwardly watching. I looked away—down the stone steps and over the little fence at Diz's taxi idling on the street. The cab's flat screens glowed with an advertisement for *M: The Musical*. But other than Diz, there were no cars driving by, no people on the sidewalks, no Bend Sinister agents, and no sign of my dad. We'd been worrying ourselves sick over nothing.

Greta made a sobbing noise. "I missed you *so much*."

"Oh, Greta," her mom mumbled into her shoulder. She stopped and held Greta at arm's length. "I'm *thrilled* you came home, but is it *safe*? Did they lock up the criminals who were after you and your dad?"

We'd been so preoccupied with how we'd explain the Blood Guard to Mrs. Sustermann that we completely forgot about the phony story Greta's dad had told her—that he and Greta had been placed in witness protection by the FBI because of threats of violence from a bunch of gangsters. No wonder she was sneaking around in the dark and pulling pistols on people.

"That's why we're here," Greta said, wrinkling her brow. "It's kind of hard to explain."

"I'm sure it's a good story," Mrs. Sustermann said, wagging the pistol at the front door. "Come on inside."

"Please stop waving that around," Dawkins said, pushing the muzzle toward the ground.

"Oh, this fake thing." Mrs. Sustermann dropped it onto the dirty welcome mat. "It's just a paperweight." She dug around in her pocket for her keys. "I don't like guns, but what with Gaspar and Greta in witness protection, and then that cab idling there for so long, I needed *some* way to defend myself." She looked at Dawkins and raised an eyebrow. "What's the sword for?"

"Stabbing and slashing, mostly," he said, raising it up, then guiding it back into his scabbard.

"Wouldn't be much help against a gun," Mrs. Sustermann said.

"You'd be surprised." Dawkins broke out into a huge smile. "A pleasure to meet you at last, Mrs. Sustermann. My name is Jack Dawkins, and we are here on an urgent matter. We need you to immediately—"

"Hello, Ronan," Mrs. Sustermann interrupted, frowning at me. "Surprised to see you here. I suppose you're in witness protection, too?"

"Um, no," I said.

"None of us are in witness protection," Greta said.

"So your father lied."

"Dad didn't exactly lie," Greta said. "It's complicated."

"I bet," said her mom.

"Please, Mrs. Sustermann," Dawkins said, stepping in front of her. "As I was saying, I am working with your husband, Gaspar. He sent us to fetch you to join him and your daughter, as Brooklyn is no longer safe."

Mrs. Sustermann unlocked the door. "You can tell me all about it over coffee."

"Alas," Dawkins said, taking her elbow, "there's no time. We will collect your things later, when it's less dangerous."

Mrs. Sustermann swept her arm out at the nighttime street. "Do you see any threats out there? I don't—aside from that cab you four came here in."

"The danger isn't one you'll see coming," Dawkins said.

Greta grabbed her mother's hand. "Jack's telling the truth. He's my friend, and Dad's friend, and you have to trust him."

"We really must go right away," Dawkins said.

Mrs. Sustermann stared at him, smiled at Greta, and said, "Okay." Then she opened the door, reached in to grab her purse, and made some kissing noises. A gray-and-white cat trotted out of the shadows. It was wearing a chunky jeweled collar that didn't really match up with anything I knew about Mrs. Sustermann—but then, people and their cats are something I've never understood.

"Come on, Grendel," Mrs. Sustermann said,

scooping the cat up and slinging him over her shoulder. "We're going for a little ride."

"Hi, Grendel!" Greta said, reaching forward and scratching the fur on either side of his snout. He purred. "I've missed you, little man!"

The cat pressed his head into her hand.

"Must we bring the cat?" Dawkins asked, hooking the collar with his pinkie and examining it.

"You have the Dobermans," Greta said. "Why shouldn't we have Grendel?"

"Fair enough," Dawkins said, nodding. "We can't leave behind family members, even when they're animals. Grab the animal's carrying case and let's go."

"Oh, Grendel can't be caged," Mrs. Sustermann said. "He's a free spirit."

"Of course he is," Dawkins said, sighing. "Please: we really *are* in a hurry."

Greta and her mom descended the steps, followed by me and Sammy. Dawkins brought up the rear, his hand resting on the hilt of his sword.

As we closed the front gate, Diz suddenly stepped on the gas. The taxi rocketed away.

"There's your danger," Mrs. Sustermann said, clucking her tongue. "New York taxi drivers."

"Where's she going?" Sammy asked.

"Oh, for the love of all that's good," Dawkins said, dragging us down behind a parked van. "She must have spotted a threat." At the far end of the street, the taxi braked hard and spun sideways, blocking the road.

But nothing happened. The cab just sat like that, the advertisements playing brightly across the flat screens on the doors and top.

"Doesn't look like anyone's th—" I started to say when two black SUVs pulled to a halt on the other side of the cab. I didn't need to look through a Verity Glass to know who was driving.

Dawkins' sword scraped loose from its scabbard. "The Bend Sinister."

CHAPTER 4
THE DOOR BETWEEN WORLDS

With a deafening *whuuuuuup!* Diz's cab exploded into light.

The burst was so dazzlingly bright that I fell back on my butt and blinked for a second before I could see again. "Did she— Is she—?"

"Did her cab just blow up?" Sammy asked.

"Not a chance," Dawkins said. "Diz is not one for that whole kamikaze thing. No, that was a strategic overload of those flat screen panels on her cab—doubtless one of the defense mechanisms she installed."

"Why would a cab do that?" Mrs. Sustermann asked, rising up for a better look.

Dawkins yanked her back down. "That blast of light and sound was an attempt to incapacitate our enemies and buy us time to escape." He took our hands and linked them together. "Everyone stay behind these parked cars. If we can get away without being seen, they may think we're still in the house." Bent low, he swiftly led us along the sidewalk away from Greta's house.

"The subway!" Greta said. "It's on the next block over! We can get there easy."

Dawkins suddenly raised his arms. We stopped behind a parked pickup truck.

"Two more vehicles. One there on that corner—" He pointed at a dark red SUV illegally idling in front of a fire hydrant. Shadowy figures sat inside it. "And a second, farther down the street." Another SUV, with another three figures inside. "I'm afraid we're surrounded. There may be no way out but to fight."

"Maybe not," I said, recognizing the house to our left. "Just follow me. And be nice."

ArmaGideon opened the basement door himself. It's where his console games were set up, and I figured he'd be there like usual. He was a big kid but not in a way anyone would find threatening; he was just a little overweight. He was wearing a Fallout T-shirt and shorts and holding a wad of bills.

"DorkLord?" he said. "I mean, Ronan—Ronan Truelove?" I almost laughed at the look on his face— that whole dropped-jaw, wide-eyes expression that you never believe happens in real life until someone does it in front of you. "You totally vanished, dude—not just from ILZ but from school and the neighborhood, too!"

"ArmaGideon!" I said. "Am I happy to see you!" During fifth and sixth grade, Gideon and I had defeated hordes of zombies, won the World Cup tons of times, and saved the universe from alien scourges on a weekly basis.

"Just Gideon," he said. "I thought you were the pizza delivery guy."

"I wish," Dawkins said from behind me. "I could murder a pizza or two right about now."

I walked in through the open door and everyone hurried in behind me. "Oh, hey—you know Greta, right? And that's Sammy, and Greta's mom, and the guy with the sword is Jack."

The basement was dark except for the light from an enormous sixty-inch television. Frozen on the screen was some sort of attack by living dead creatures.

"Wow," Gideon said, staring at Greta. "I can't believe the smartest girl in school is here, standing inside my game room."

"Don't let it go to your head," Greta muttered.

Gideon eyeballed the sword in Dawkins' hand as he eased the door shut. "*Cool*." Then he noticed the cat Mrs. Sustermann still held over her shoulder. "Okay, Truelove, why don't you tell me what's going on."

"Really sorry to barge in," I said, thinking fast, "but you're the only one who can help. We're playing the heroes in a crazy intense real-world game called the Blood Guard."

45

He made a fist. "Dang, you finally got in on an ARG!" Gideon was eager to play ARGs, alternate reality games set up using real locations. We'd always talked about joining a team and competing but never managed to pull it off—mostly because we were too young and too broke. "So *that's* why that guy's got the fake sword." He reached out for it.

Dawkins held it out of reach and said, "Sorry, but this is, um—"

"It's a prize he got for completing a side quest," I said. "Rule is only the victor can use the sword. Just like the cat Mrs. Sustermann is carrying."

"The cat was a prize, too?" Gideon asked.

"It's a pretty weird ARG," I said. "Anyway, we need to get off your street. Another team—really vicious players—have set up traps at the ends of the block. They have guns that shoot bolts of lightning, and all we have is that one dinky sword and the cat for our defense."

"You guys are so dead!" Gideon blew out a loud breath.

"I was hoping you could help us this time, and next time, you can play in place of Mrs. Sustermann."

"Oh, absolutely," Mrs. Sustermann said, petting Grendel. "This really isn't my kind of game at all. Monopoly is more my speed."

Gideon nodded. "You can count on me, Truelove."

"Don't I know it," I said, resting my hand on his shoulder. "Is the Door still open?"

"The Door Between Worlds? It will *never* be closed!" he said, pumping his fist in the air. "But let's do this fast. I don't want to miss my pizza."

• • •

At the back of Gideon's yard was a six-foot-tall wood fence overgrown with ivy. Gideon took us to one corner. "The latch is under all those plants," he said. "I haven't been through it in a couple years."

Dawkins fished his hand around in the ivy, said, "Ah-ha!" and then something *clonked* and the corner of the fence swung outward.

On the other side was a strip of land that ran between the fences of two backyards, between neighboring brownstones, and all the way to the next street.

We looked at each other. It was pretty narrow.

"Too tight for *me*," Gideon said, shrugging. "But you all should fit if you walk sideways."

"Then that is what we shall do. Thank you!" Dawkins turned and scooched through, leading with his sword hand.

Greta went next, and then her mom, holding Grendel, and then Sammy.

"That is one sweet setup," Sammy told Gideon. "I wish we could have hung out and played a few games." He slipped through the gate.

"Come back anytime!" Gideon called after him.

Before I left, I said, "I really owe you, Gideon. You're saving our lives here."

"Aw, it's just a game," he said, sweeping his hand through the air.

I looked down the narrow alley—my friends were already far along—and then grabbed Gideon's arm. "It's *not* a game," I whispered. "It's *real*. And those people out there will kill us. Or you. Promise me you won't open your door to anyone, and that you won't go outside for any reason."

"Geez, Ronan," Gideon said, pulling away. "If you don't want me to join your ARG, you could just say that."

From Gideon's house, his mom called his name.

"The pizza guy is probably here," he said.

"Gideon," I pleaded, "I'm *not* kidding around. We're being hunted. And the people after us are ruthless. Please make sure it really *is* the pizza guy before you open the door. And if it's not, call the police."

Then I, too, scooted through the Door Between Worlds.

When I emerged, Dawkins, Greta, her mom, and Sammy were waiting, crouched down between two parked cars. Everyone but the cat looked filthy.

I'd forgotten how dirty it was in the passageway; my clothes were smeared with greasy soot, and my hands were scratched and bleeding in a few places from the sharp edges of the bricks.

"What took you so long?" Greta whispered.

"I had to warn Gideon," I said. "We can't have him going outside and bumping into the Bend Sinister."

"Good man," Dawkins said, clapping me on the back. "The coast is clear." Sixty feet away were the subway's half-green, half-white globe lights that I'd noticed on the drive earlier.

Within seconds, we had descended the stairs and were off the street.

"But what about Diz?" Greta asked.

"What is a Diz?" her mother asked.

"A person," Greta said. "You'd like her."

"She's hell on wheels, is our Diz," Dawkins said, examining the ceiling-to-floor turnstiles. "She can take care of herself."

"She's like you, right?" Sammy asked. "An Overseer?"

Dawkins shook his head. "If you mean in terms of my particular healing talents . . . no. Diz is a rank-and-file Blood Guard. If she gets killed, she stays that way."

Mrs. Sustermann raised an eyebrow. "Don't *all* people who get killed 'stay that way'?"

"You'd be surprised," Dawkins said, fussing with the turnstile.

"So you keep saying."

"*Mom*," Greta said. "I'll explain later."

"These spinning cage things are beyond me," Dawkins said. "How does anyone hop the turnstiles anymore?"

"They don't," Mrs. Sustermann said. She held up a flimsy plastic MetroCard. "But don't worry, I've got you covered."

Our end of the station was empty, but there were twenty or so people scattered along the platform, and way down at the other end a half-dozen old guys in mismatched suit jackets and bowlers started warbling "You Are My Sunshine."

"What's that about?" Sammy asked.

"Just some folks singing for spare change," Mrs. Sustermann said, sitting down on a bench. Greta sat beside her, and Sammy went over to study the maps and the white-tiled walls.

"So my dad must have told the Bend Sinister," I said, stepping closer to Dawkins. "Before he was thrown out, he must have told them about Greta."

"Else why would they show up here, right?" Dawkins whispered. "Except . . . there are hundreds of Bend Sinister in the city. Why wouldn't they have kidnapped Greta's mom before now?"

A gentle wind began to blow through the station— air forced ahead of a train. "The subway's coming," I said.

"And not a moment too soon," Dawkins said. "We

managed to pull this one out of the fire, thanks to your pal Gideon back there."

At that moment, three pairs of black-suited legs appeared at the top of the steps, slowly descending until we were face-to-face through the turnstile gate with three Bend Sinister agents—the bald man and the two women from the heliport.

The bald guy was eating a slice of pizza.

I stepped up to the black metal bars. "Where'd you get that?"

He chewed and smiled and said nothing.

Dawkins hooked his arm across my chest and pulled me back. "No need to stand so close, Ronan."

The redhead raised her hands and began whispering something, and the curved chrome bars of the turnstile cage started to glow. How long until they were soft enough to bend aside?

The other, dark-haired woman wiggled her fingers in a wave. "I'd hoped we would meet again before the night ended—and here you are!"

"Would love to stay and chat," Dawkins said, raising his voice over the screech of the arriving train. He pointed his thumb over his shoulder at the long silver subway car. "But we don't want to miss our ride."

"Tell me," asked the woman, reaching forward and bending one of the turnstile bars backward, "why are you and Head Truelove so interested in the Sustermann woman?"

"Why are *you* so interested?" Dawkins asked.

A *bing-bong* sounded, the doors opened, and all of us stepped inside the car.

"Because you are!" the bald man shouted. He and the dark-haired woman bent back one bar after another, their hands sizzling as they grasped the hot metal.

And then the doors closed, and the train rolled forward, slowly picking up speed until it carried us away into the dark tunnel.

CHAPTER 5

A SONG IN HIS HEART,
A SWORD IN HIS HAND

I collapsed into a seat right by the door, relieved that we'd escaped.

Dawkins eased into the seat next to me, care fully slipping his cutlass out of sight beneath our bench.

Greta's mom plopped onto the three-seat bench across from us, and Greta sat right next to her mom. They put their heads together over the cat, who curled up on the seat between them.

"That is the calmest kitty I have ever seen," Dawkins said.

"Grendel can be a monster now and then," Mrs. Sustermann said, scratching the cat's ears. "But generally he is at peace with the world."

"This subway is kind of janky," Sammy commented, eyeballing the walls, poles, and advertisements.

"This is an old car," I said. "The newer ones are tons nicer."

The seats were made from this ugly orange plastic and came in three-seaters that hugged the walls, and two-seaters that stuck out into the center, forming big Ls like the saddest bunch of Tetris blocks in the world. I stared down at the floor, which was made out of a single giant piece of tan linoleum and had all sorts of disgusting stains on it.

We were in the empty front half of the car. Nearby were an old couple with a pushcart full of groceries and a couple of older teens, and at the back were three women who talked loud and laughed a lot.

"Mission accomplished, guys!" Sammy spun around on the metal pole between us. "We got out of there *and* no one got hurt."

Was that true? I couldn't get that slice of pizza out of my mind.

Just then, the train tilted and the wheels shrieked through a turn. The fluorescents above us stuttered and went dark. A second later, they came back on.

Sammy pointed at a red wooden handle dangling from the ceiling. Behind it was a sign reading EMER-GENCY BRAKE. "Does that old-school thing really stop the train?"

"Let's not find out," Dawkins said. "Leave it alone."

"Okay, okay! I'm going to go check out the rest of the car," Sammy said, then swung from pole to pole down to where the three women sat.

But I was barely watching. I have never felt so guilty in my life. "I'm worried about Gideon," I said.

"We don't know that anything bad happened to him," Dawkins whispered. "Just because someone's eating—"

"*Really?* It's just a big coincidence?"

He looked away. "Of course not. I hope that he and his family are okay. He helped us escape, and our leaving the Bend Sinister at his door was poor thanks."

"Some escape. What if they run after us?" I asked. "I was on a train before and a Bend Sinister guy chased it. He ran like sixty miles an hour. And subways are tons slower than that train."

"Could happen," Dawkins admitted, "but we had a head start, and running along train tracks in a dark tunnel is no easy task. And they'll have no idea if we got off at any other stop along the way . . . such as this one."

The brakes whined sharply as the train rattled into a station. A bunch of noisy young people got on at the back. Then the doors closed and we were off again.

"Did you catch that last thing the Hand said through his surrogate?" Dawkins asked.

Again the car was plunged into darkness. And then the overhead lights flickered back on.

"They came after Mrs. Sustermann because we did," I said quietly.

"So that group now likely thinks she is a Pure."

"That's good, right?" I asked. "They're confused."

"No, Ronan, that's *bad*. What if they kidnap her, or kill her, or bonk her over the head with the Damascene 'Scope?"

I stared across at Greta and her mom. They looked so happy, forehead to forehead, like two girls at a slumber party telling each other secrets. Greta thought she and her mom were safe. But all we'd done was double the amount of trouble coming their way.

"And my dad is still out there, and he for sure knows."

"Right. And he's likely desperate to nab Greta as a replacement soul for the Pure he lost—the one he was supposed to deliver to Evangeline Birk and the Bend Sinister." He slapped my knee. "But don't look so glum, Ronan. We'll meet up with Diz and go hide out in Agatha's swanky penthouse apartment as planned. And then tomorrow the rest of the Blood Guard will arrive, and everything will be hunky-dory."

The more confident Dawkins seemed, the less I believed him.

The train slowed into another station and a group of people got off our car. I craned my head around to watch through the window, waiting for those Bend Sinister agents to pop up on the platform.

But they never did. Soon the train got moving again.

When I turned back around, Sammy was right in front of me.

"I checked out the car in front of this one. Just a bunch of sleepy people and an old guy with ratty dreads strumming a guitar and singing 'No Woman, No Cry.'"

"If you don't mind, Sammy," Dawkins said, "please stay in *this* car. I'd rather we not lose you."

"You have my word that I will stay in this car," Sammy said, crossing his heart with his index finger. And then he swung from center pole to center pole all the way to the back door.

You're missing something, you idiot, I thought, remembering my dream.

"Why?" I wondered aloud. "Why does it matter if my dad brings a soul to this Birk lady? What is she going to do with it—start a collection?" I rubbed the scar on my palm and remembered the open aluminum packing case in Agatha's greenhouse, the freezing-cold Conceptacle inside that held Flavia's soul. "The whole point of their plan was to take souls out of circulation so that they can't be reincarnated, right? So why carry it around? Why not just dump the Conceptacle into a pit where it won't ever be found?"

The door at the far end of the car opened, and both Dawkins and I looked up. The six old guys in bowler hats paraded in.

Five carried canes, and all of them were dressed in mismatched suits, some of the coats turned inside out. A couple seemed ashamed to be performing for coins and stared down at their feet. But the one in the front removed his hat, held it between his hands, and announced, "We are going to sing a song for you tonight, one you probably all know." He cleared his throat.

Dawkins turned back to me. "That is a very good question. Why *did* your dad bring that Pure soul to the Glass estate? Why not leave it somewhere safe? We'd been thinking he was just being foolish, but that's . . . too easy."

I shook my head. "My dad is a lot of things, but foolish isn't one of them."

"So he brought it deliberately. Why?"

The man at the back of the group, his head dropped against his chest, flattened his hand against his ratty brown coat and started making noises that sounded like a bass guitar. The other four hummed along as the leader began. The song had strange lyrics—about a shark biting someone and blood billowing, and it took me a full verse before I recognized the tune.

Sammy slid into the pair of seats facing us. "What *is* this weird song? They should go back to 'You Are My Sunshine.'"

"It's called 'Mack the Knife,'" I said. "It's a song about a murderer from an old German opera. My dad played classical stuff like that all the time."

As they sang, they shuffled forward in tiny half steps, like most subway buskers, moving slowly so that they didn't reach the other end of the car before their song ended. Two of the men shook plastic cups full of change. A few people dropped in coins, but almost everyone else ignored them.

Greta's mom slowly swung her foot in time.

The train braked into another station, the doors opened, and the men froze in place while passengers got on and off.

That's a weird move, I thought.

But then they picked up the song again right where they'd stopped once the train departed.

The fluorescents overhead buzzed and blinked off, then buzzed again and came back on.

"I really wish the lights would stop doing that," I said.

"It just means the cars went over a switch or a gap in the third rail," Greta said. "Like when you enter a tunnel."

"Of course you would know that," I said. Greta may be a Pure and my friend, but she was also the smartest student at my school and sometimes kind of annoying about it.

Greta shrugged. "I can't help it that I actually learn things."

"So we're in a tunnel now?" Sammy asked.

"Yeah," I said. "We're somewhere under the East River."

"Wild!" he said. "How much water you think is over our heads?"

I tipped my head back and stared at the ceiling, imagining it. "A lot?"

"Thanks for the *illuminating* answer." Sammy got up and wandered toward the front of the car again.

Dawkins had been thinking while we chattered. "He brought it to Agatha's place *because* the Damascene 'Scope was there. Because of what it can do."

I thought about the weird, Victorian-era device. The Damascene 'Scope looked like a mix between a telescope and a big brass cannon, but all I'd ever seen it do was good. First, when we accidentally used it to purify Agatha, and the second time, when we saved Flavia. "We used the 'Scope and the Glass Gauntlet to restore Flavia's soul. But why would my dad want to project a Pure soul into someone else?"

"That's only one of its uses. Agatha mentioned another use that I hadn't really thought about until now."

"What's that?" I asked.

"She said it could *destroy* souls, could eradicate them. Permanently."

The singers had reached the middle of the car, and the sad truth is that they'd sounded a whole lot better when they'd been far away. Not that it mattered to Mrs. Sustermann; she dug around in her purse and took out a folded dollar bill. She pinched it between two fingers and waved it at the guys, and they did their strange little shuffle between the seats toward our section.

I glanced from Greta's mom to the lead singer, but as I did, I glimpsed the soft jawline of the last of the performers, one who'd kept his head down the whole time.

And I recognized it.

I clutched Dawkins' arm. "It's *him*."

"Guard Greta," Dawkins whispered, then bent forward, grabbed the cutlass from under the seat, and rolled off the bench to the center of the car.

My dad pushed back the brim of his hat, looked straight into my eyes, and smiled at the same moment as the five men around him drew long, thin swords out of the wooden canes.

"Son," he said.

And then the lights went out.

CHAPTER 6
GUARDING GRETA

The train slammed to a halt, and I was thrown to the floor. From the shouts around me, I guessed I wasn't the only one—someone had yanked the emergency brake.

I crawled forward in the dark, blindly sweeping my hands back and forth, trying to find Greta.

From behind me came the clang of swords striking each other—Dawkins, holding off my dad's Bend Sinister team. And I could hear people shouting all up and down the car. One man hollered, "Everyone calm down!" Another voice answered him, saying, "*You* calm down—I don't want to die on the Four train!" And then total chaos.

All the noise made it hard to think.

Guard Greta, Dawkins had commanded, like that was easy. *I couldn't even* see *Greta*.

And then I remembered Diz tapping her sunglasses and saying her Verity Glass worked like night-vision goggles. *Thanks, Diz.* I reached into my shirt, yanked my glass up on its chain, and wedged it over my right eye.

Immediately I could see Greta sprawled across the floor of the car.

She was pretty much *all* I could see.

That's the thing about Pures: when seen through a Verity Glass, their souls blaze with a searingly bright light—almost painful to behold. Greta's soul was so dazzling that I had to turn away or be blinded.

When I did, I discovered something else: her light *illuminated* the other souls in the car. It was like everyone else's soul burned a little brighter because of the nearness of a Pure. Through the lens, the subway was a dark violet, but I could see people cowering in their seats at the back of the car, trying to avoid getting hurt by the swordplay taking place ten feet away from me.

Unlike everyone else, the Bend Sinister agents were only the faintest of shimmery outlines, barely there at all. They'd given up their life force when they'd joined the Bend Sinister. Except for my dad. His soul was all there. The only thing he'd given up when he joined the Bend Sinister was his family.

Dawkins had the agents trapped in the cramped space where two rows of seats extended out into the center of the car; there was only a narrow passage between the benches, and he and his sword were blocking the way.

Somehow he was able to fight them in the dark, blocking their attacks without seeing them. Twice one of them tried to clamber over the seats, but somehow Dawkins sensed it. Each time, he swept his blade or his leg out and knocked the guy back, then brought his sword up to block the attacks of the other men.

But he wouldn't be able to keep them there forever.

Greta's mom was lying low on the row of seats where she'd been sitting, saying, "Greta?" over and over, and reaching toward Greta's empty seat with one arm while clutching the cat to her chest with the other. (I could also see Grendel—I guess cats have souls, too.)

Guard Greta, Dawkins had instructed me, so I crawled across the filthy floor toward the light. When I was close enough to hear Greta's breathing, I reached out and touched her shoulder.

Her fist clocked me right in the jaw.

"Hey!" I said, falling backward.

"Ronan?" Greta whispered. "Sorry!"

"I'm trying to *help*," I said, taking her hand. "This way." I led her forward on our hands and knees.

"Ronan!" she whispered. "We have to get my mom!"

"Dawkins will protect her," I said. "You need to get under these seats." There was a row of three on the wall and nothing under them.

"No *way*," she said.

So I pushed her. Hard.

"Stop that!"

The one nice thing about the dirty linoleum was that Greta slid pretty easily. She struggled, but I wedged my foot against one of the poles and shoved, then blocked her with my body. With my left shoulder against the bottom edge of the seats and my right shoulder flat on the floor, she was completely hidden.

"*Ronan!*" Her fists pounded my back. "Get *off!*"

"Shh," I said. "We don't want them to find us."

Hiding under the seats meant I couldn't really see what was going on anymore. But I could still *hear* things.

Sometime during our crawl, the riders had stopped shouting, which made the clashing of the swords sound that much louder.

"Evelyn?" my dad called. "Where'd you go, son?"

I kept quiet and hoped he didn't look down.

Suddenly Dawkins yelled out in pain. "They got past!" Somebody shouted and a cat yowled.

"Grendel!" Greta pushed against me. "He's with my mom."

Feet pounded past in a run.

A mechanical noise from the front of the car—the connecting door opening and closing?—made me turn that way. I looked just in time to be blinded by a flare of red light. Metal sizzled, and sparks rained down to the floor in the dark. Then I could hear the train starting up

66

again and rolling away down the tracks.

Except we weren't moving at all.

The car was silent. After a moment, I heard a lighter strike, and a flame appeared.

"They've run off," Dawkins said. He held his Zippo high. "Ronan? Greta? Sammy? Mrs. Sustermann? Is everyone present and accounted for?"

I slid out, relieved. I'd kept Greta safe.

"Come on," I said, reaching back to help her out from the bench.

She smacked my hand away and stood up on her own. "Don't talk to me."

"Me and Greta are down here," I said.

"I'm over here," Sammy said.

A flashlight beam appeared at the rear of the train, and a conductor came into the car. "Okay, who's the wise guy who pulled the emergency brake?" she asked. She raked the light across the riders cowering on the floor, then pointed it at Dawkins. "What happened here?"

"We were attacked," Dawkins said. "A group of men . . . Are the lights going to come back on?"

"Any moment now," the conductor said. She slowly swept the beam up and down. "Sir," she said, "you have—sticking out of you—are those *swords*?"

Dawkins looked down. "Hardly! These are only *foils*—skinny little blades, more stabby than anything." He withdrew first one, then a second, and finally the third, dropping each to the ground. "See? They didn't hit anything vital."

The lights overhead strobed twice. The third time, they stayed on.

In the center of the car, Dawkins stood panting, his clothes bloody. Three of the cane-handled foils lay on the floor. I knew that even as I watched, his wounds would be sealing themselves up.

The conductor gasped and covered her mouth. "I'll call the hospital."

"It looks much worse than it is!" he told the woman. He opened his shirt. "See? There's not even a wound."

Fifteen feet away in the other direction, toward the front of the car, Sammy was crouched in the L of two rows of seats. In his hand was the red wooden emergency brake pull.

Dawkins looked around wildly. "Where's your mum, Greta?"

Greta shoved me aside. "Mom?" she shouted. "*Mom?*"

On the floor behind Dawkins was an overturned bowler and a sprinkling of coins. Next to them, still folded, was a one-dollar bill.

"Mom!" Greta screamed.

Dawkins blurred as he pounded past Greta to the front of the car. He strained to turn the handle of the connecting door, but nothing happened. "They've *welded* it shut somehow," he said. "No matter." He took a step back, grabbed the bar above a row of seats, and swung his feet into the subway window.

The glass popped out of its rubber molding and fell to the tracks outside.

"Hey!" said the conductor. "You can't do that!"

But Dawkins was already gone. He'd leaped through the window and disappeared into the dark.

• • •

Greta wouldn't look at me, just sat on the bench where her mom had been sitting and shivered.

"Is she going to be okay?" the conductor asked. "None of you are hurt, are you?"

"No, ma'am," I said.

"It was me who pulled the brake," Sammy said. "When I saw their swords, I just thought . . . It seemed like a good idea."

"That's okay, son," the woman said. "I'd have done the same." She looked back at the cane swords on the ground. "And none of you know *why* these gentlemen attacked your friend? Nor how they made off with the rest of the train?"

We shook our heads.

The conductor leaned out the window and then brought her head back in. "The front car's been decoupled!" she said into a walkie-talkie on her shoulder. "They were using *swords*—and they stabbed a kid. He's the one that ran away."

While a half dozen transit workers examined the tracks outside the train, two men remounted the window Dawkins had kicked out.

And then the subway started moving again.

"Didn't they take the engine car?" Sammy asked.

"Nah, any one of these cars can function as the engine. They're all tied to the third rail." The conductor smiled. "Listen, I've got to go talk to the police. My name is Letitia. I'll find you at the City Hall station and take your statements there, okay?"

"Okay," I said, and watched her walk through the connecting door at the rear of the car.

I turned to Greta. "I'm really— We couldn't— How was I supposed to . . ." Nothing I could think to say was the right thing. "I'm sorry, I'm sorry! I messed up."

But she wouldn't say a word, just pulled the hood of her sweatshirt over her head and turned her face away.

When the subway limped into the Brooklyn Bridge–City Hall station, we disembarked along with everyone else who had been on the train. The platform went from empty to full in about three seconds. Most of the passengers were angry. A thick crowd surrounded Letitia the conductor.

"Now what do we do?" Sammy asked.

Across from us, an empty downtown 6 train sat on the local track. The words LAST STOP glowed from the sign in the window. From its speakers, a recording

70

repeated, "This is the last stop on the train. Please exit the train. This is the last stop on the train . . ."

Dawkins' head popped up behind one of the windows.

"Um, guys," I said, jostling Sammy.

Dawkins waved his hand once and then disappeared again.

"What?" Sammy asked.

"Jack. He's on that train across the platform."

Sammy turned and said, "I don't see anyone."

Dawkins popped up again and waved us over.

"Come on," I said, steering Greta by the elbow. She shook me off.

We got on board just as the doors started to close.

"I thought you three would *never* get here," Dawkins said.

"But this is the last stop," I protested.

"Only for the unwitting," Dawkins said. "All of you get down so that conductor and her police officer friends don't catch sight of you."

The three of us sat next to Dawkins on the floor.

"Sorry to have abandoned you back there. I had to try and rescue Mrs. Sustermann," Dawkins said, "but they had too great a lead, and by the time I caught up, they'd already abandoned that disconnected car."

"You didn't protect my mom," Greta said, staring straight ahead at nothing.

"No," Dawkins said. "And I'm deeply sorry for that,

Greta. But I give you my word we will get her back."

"Sure," Greta said.

"They grabbed the cat, too," I said.

"Truelove and his team must have ended up on that subway platform the same way we did: hiding from the Bend Sinister. But then they got lucky: we showed up with just the person they'd been looking for."

He meant Greta, I knew, but I also knew Greta would think he meant her mom.

The train started moving. It slowly left the station and entered a dark tunnel.

"Is this going to take us to Agatha's?" I asked.

"No," Dawkins said. "This really is the end of the line. But the train follows an old turnaround loop and comes out on the opposite track to go uptown. We, however, will be gone before it arrives there."

We entered a sharp curve, the wheels shrieking against the tracks. And then the train ground to a halt.

The doors opened onto darkness.

"This is our stop," Dawkins said. "Everybody off."

CHAPTER 7
CAT-O-GRAPHY

The moment we exited, the doors sighed shut and the train started up again, the shrilling of the wheels on the tracks so loud I had to cover my ears.

We were in some kind of subway station, that much was obvious: there was the same foot-wide band of neon yellow marking the edge of the platform, and that feeling you get in large spaces—an inkling that the darkness around you is *big*.

Dawkins raised a palm. "Wait here a moment." He waved at a man in one of the driver's booths, who waved back.

"A buddy of yours?" I asked.

"Blood Guard," Dawkins said. "Retired, like Diz. Stops the Six train for us when we need to drop in." He walked away into the dark. "Wait here while I get the lights."

We were alone, listening to the racket of the train as it slowly went into a tunnel and vanished. I looked up. I couldn't be sure, but I thought I could see the sky through a window overhead. "Is that a skylight?" I asked.

At that moment, dozens of old-fashioned incandescent bulbs came to life.

"Now *this* is more like it!" Sammy said, looking around and clapping. "Why aren't *all* the stations like this?"

We were in the coolest subway station I've ever seen.

Which isn't saying a whole lot, because thanks to the rats, trash, graffiti, and four or five million people who use them every day, New York City's subways can get pretty nasty. But this place was nothing like a regular station.

Even Greta came out of her funk long enough to mutter, "Wow."

The platform curved around like a crescent moon, and over it were a dozen multicolored archways, like beautiful ribs over the tracks. Parts of the walls were covered in tile—the usual white tile you see everywhere on the New York subway, but also bottle green, burnt orange, silvery gray, brick red, and cobalt blues. High above, the light glinted off of glass—the skylights I'd seen in the dark.

It was . . . *grand*—that's the word for it. In some weird way, it reminded me of being in a church.

In the dead center of the platform was a broad staircase. Above it was a fancy tiled archway with the words CITY HALL set in stone.

"Are we going to see the mayor?" Sammy asked. "Is *he* in the Blood Guard?"

"Absolutely not," Dawkins said, glancing back. "That staircase just goes to the old closed-up City Hall entrance. Our destination is this way." We followed the curve of the platform, Dawkins talking and gesturing as he walked. "This was the original City Hall subway station, designed in nineteen-oh-something-or-other by a bunch of guys who usually made cathedrals, and ended up building things like Mount Rushmore. But the city got too big, needed bigger stations, so this little gem was closed down on the final day of 1945. Now it's used only as a turnaround for the Six train."

"That's a bummer," Sammy said. "A station this awesome should be seen by people."

Along the wall at the edge of the platform were steps down to a gray metal door. Dawkins tapped a code into a keypad, the door unlocked, and he ushered us inside.

"Everything was shut down except for this control center, where they monitored the entire subway line until the nineteen seventies. And then it, too, became obsolete and was closed." He slapped some switches, and rows of naked fluorescent bulbs buzzed and lit up.

The room was wide and deep, but somehow still claustrophobic. Maybe because of the super-low ceiling, or maybe because of the thick fur of dust covering everything. The walls were full of yellowed memos and calendars and pictures of people who had probably been dead since the end of the last century, and the floor was filled by rows of gray metal desks. At the front of the room were painted maps of the subway system, with the different lines indicated by big colored bulbs.

"It's like some kind of postapocalyptic zombie video game world," I said. "Or a museum of boringness."

"Is the air in here even safe to breathe?" Sammy covered his mouth.

"Sure!" Dawkins sucked in a big lungful and then sneezed. "Just avoid the dirty parts of the room. There's a mopped path on the floor right along the edge here." He carefully picked his way through the trash on a clean strip of mottled black linoleum, and we followed.

In a pristine corner were four desks from this century—sleek and clean—outfitted with new computers that purred in sleep mode. Bolted above them were five widescreen monitors and a router.

"Why don't you guys ever work in *new* places?" Sammy asked.

"The Blood Guard prefers to be surrounded by history," Dawkins said.

"More like the Blood Guard prefers to save money. Abandoned sites are cheap," I said.

"And also anonymous," Dawkins said. "This is the Blood Guard way station for Manhattan. Diz will know to check in here when she can't raise us on the phone. And while we wait for her, we are going to track down—"

"Does this godawful hole have a restroom?" Greta asked. "I need a bathroom."

"Through there," Dawkins said, pointing down another mopped-clean strip. At its far end was a narrow set of steps. "I'm sure it's clean, but fair warning: the facilities date from 1905 or thereabouts, so don't expect fancy."

Without another word, Greta marched across the room and disappeared. The sound of a door latching carried across the musty room.

It was time to call for help; and that meant calling my mom. The Guard were still a few hours away, but that didn't mean we shouldn't bring them up to speed so that they could come to our aid as soon as they arrived. I took out my cell phone.

But there was no signal.

"There's no cell phone service?" I said.

Dawkins looked at his phone. "I don't see any bars, so . . . I suppose not."

"Poor Greta," Sammy said. He rolled a chair back from a desk and sat in it. "This whole operation is such a mess."

"I know," Dawkins said, tapping at the keyboards and waking up the computers. "But we *will* get her mom back."

"What I don't understand," I said, "is why my dad took her mom in the first place. I mean, we were *all* there. Why grab Greta's mom?"

"Because in the dark, he thought she was Greta, obviously," Sammy said. He opened up a browser on the computer. "We have Internet service down here. Is there wifi, or are these computers hard-wired into the net?"

"Why would he want Greta?" Dawkins broke into a wide, skeptical smile. "More likely Mrs. Sustermann was the easier target, Sammy."

"Come *on*," Sammy whispered, "how stupid do you think I am? He wasn't after Greta's mom; he was after *Greta*. Because she's a . . ." He fluttered his hands in the air and mouthed the word *Pure*.

"Keep that theory to yourself," Dawkins said, pointing at him.

Across the room, a toilet flushed.

"Theory," Sammy repeated. "Right. Anyway, Greta and her mom are the same size, they were both wearing hoodies, her mom was sitting where Greta had been before the lights went out . . . he just made a mistake."

Greta came back out, red-eyed. Something had changed; she didn't look shell-shocked anymore.

She looked angry.

"What were you guys whispering about?" she asked.

"Your mom," I said. "We're going to find her, don't worry."

"Is that supposed to be reassuring, Ronan?" Greta asked, jabbing a finger in my chest. "Because I *am* worried. What's the great plan now—to sit in this rank old subway station and hope she shows up?"

"Um, probably not," I said.

"This old subway station *is* key to finding her." Dawkins tapped one of the flat screens, which now showed a coiled mess of colored lines. After a moment I realized it was the subway system. "We're going to use the transit computer network to find your mum's cat." He typed something into another of the keyboards, and a second flat screen woke up and started cycling through images of people standing around on subway platforms and boarding trains, and even of trains barreling through tunnels. Live feeds from all over the city.

"Grendel?" Greta snorted. "Your genius plan to rescue my mom is to find her cat?"

"That hideous jeweled collar Grendel wears," Dawkins said. "I noticed it has a charging port. Why is that?"

Greta stared at him for a moment, then laughed. "Oh gosh. It's called Cat-o-Grapher. The collar sends out a cellular ping, and Mom can log on to a website that tracks where Grendel goes in the neighborhood, or use the site to find him when he doesn't come home."

"So if we locate the cat, we locate your mom."

Greta shot up off the desk and wrapped her arms around Dawkins. "That's a great idea!"

He blushed. "Thank you. Now, if they've exited the subways, we'll get a ping no problem. But if they haven't . . . we're going to need to access the private transit network. Which is the other reason we've come here."

"What do you need me to do?" Greta asked, rolling a chair over and sitting down next to Sammy.

He opened up a log-in window. "First we'll need your mom's password to access the Cat-o-Grapher site—"

"But I don't know it!" Greta said.

"That's okay, we can figure it out," said Sammy, cracking his knuckles and typing in a Web address. "Parents never pick tough passwords. Just tell me all her personal things—favorite food, color, that sort of thing. Let's start with her middle name and birthday."

"Millicent," Greta said, "and her birthday is in a few weeks: September twenty-fourth."

Sammy's fingers flew over the keys. "No, and no. What about your birthday? What about the *cat's* birthday? Let's just make a list . . ."

Dawkins draped his arm around my shoulders and steered me over to another computer. "While they work on that, I need you to visit that gamer website where you and your dad last communicated."

"ILZ?" I said. "You think he's back on ILZ?"

"Absolutely," Dawkins said. "He will have realized very quickly that he grabbed the wrong person. So he'll want to make a trade. And he'll want to do it soon. Remember, he's desperate. The whole reason he was in that subway station was because the Bend Sinister were out in force above ground. He didn't want to be caught by them any more than we did—at least, not until he has a prize to bring them."

"Greta," I whispered.

"Greta."

"If Sammy was able to figure out Greta is a Pure," I said, watching the two of them working, "how long until Greta wises up?"

Dawkins rolled his eyes. "Oh, she'll *never* put it together. Even if it occurred to her, she'd never believe it. People are blind about themselves. For an opinion that completely misses the obvious, nothing beats self-appraisal."

I logged on and tabbed over to my mailbox. The only things in it were the email exchanges with my dad. First the ones where my mom pretended to be me. And then, later, the ones where he and I were actually writing to each other.

"There's nothing new here," I said. "It's a dead end."

"Nonsense," Dawkins said. "Send him a note. You know, 'Hi Dad, You stole my friend's mum and I want her back.' That sort of thing."

"You want me to email *that*?"

"No, Ronan," Dawkins said. "That was me making a little joke. Just keep it short." He strolled back over to Greta and Sammy. "How are you two progressing?"

"We got in easy," Sammy said, pumping his arms in victory. "Her password? Name of her first cat from when she was a kid."

"Well done! So where is the little beastie?"

"It's not really clear," Sammy said. The screen showed a street grid of lower Manhattan, bound on three sides by the blue of the water. "The last pings were an hour ago in the East River, kind of halfway between the tunnel and the Brooklyn Bridge."

"Could they have, you know, thrown the cat off the bridge and into the river?" I asked.

"Oh god." Greta gulped. "Poor Grendel."

"Probably not," Sammy said. "The website's just confused. Geolocation gets sloppy over big bodies of water. Not enough cell towers to triangulate."

I turned back to my screen.

To: Sisyphus79
From: DorkLord2K1

But after that, I had no idea what to write. *We know you have Mrs. Sustermann. Let her go—or else!* Nah. I wasn't really in a position to threaten my dad. But I wasn't going to get all chatty with him, either. We were past all that, and we both knew it. So I wrote a single line

Tell us what you want.

and before I could second guess myself, I hit Send.

Then, feeling queasy, I sat back and stared at the screen. There was a second email I had to send. I wrote it quickly.

To: *ArmaGide0n*
From: *DorkLord2K1*

Thanks again for the help, d00d. We got out of there okay, and it is all because of you. Your friend, R.

Please be alive, I wished as I hit Send.

My inbox dinged right away with a reply.

But it wasn't Gideon. It was my dad.

His email was one line, too; in fact, it was just one word.

Skype?

CHAPTER 8
A PINK FLUFFY UNICORN

"You look a little . . . green," my dad said first thing.

So did he, but I didn't tell him that. There was a faint greenish light cast on his face from below, like on a TV show villain. The dark marble walls and big flowering plants behind him only added to the eeriness.

"It's because of the fluorescent lights," I said.

"And that gray wall behind you," he said, squinting. "What are those things stuck to it—pieces of tape?"

They *were* pieces of tape. Forty-year-old tape.

My chair was parked in an empty corner of the room, balanced on a crinkly pile of office bulletins about dress codes, vacation days, fire codes, smoking areas, and a faded calendar forever stuck on August 1974. "We can't have him see any clues as to where we are," Dawkins had said, frantically tearing things off the barest wall we could find in the room.

From behind the laptop, Greta, Sammy, and Dawkins watched and gave me signals—Greta rolled her hands over each other, and Dawkins mimed cutting his throat with his finger. It was more confusing than anything, so I ignored them.

"Who cares?" I said. "Can we cut the small talk?"

"Sure, son," Dad said. He had changed his clothes since the subway. Now he was dressed in a nice dark suit and a gold tie and might have looked like a newscaster except for a long pair of scratches on his left cheek. "I assume your friends are there with you—Greta and that other kid, as well as that Overseer?"

I stared at his tie. It was a single Windsor knot—I knew that because he'd taught me how to tie one myself. I didn't want to look in his eyes, because I feared I couldn't be tough if I had to see his anger and disappointment in me. Lifelong habits die hard; even though he was an evil man, he was also my dad. "What do you *want*?" I asked.

"A simple trade," he said. "You want Mrs. Sustermann, and I want . . ."

"Me!" I shouted. My dad stopped talking, confused.

We'd been idiots to let Greta observe. He was going to demand *Greta*, and if she heard him say that, even *she* would be able to figure out why her mom had been targeted: because her daughter, Greta, is a Pure.

But what would happen after that? Would Greta

86

die? Would the world begin to end? Would she become evil like Agatha Glass had been after being zapped with the Damascene 'Scope? Dawkins had told me that if a Pure learned she was special, she would "lose that essential goodness" and stop being a Pure, but what did that even mean?

Dawkins must have been thinking the same thing, because he raised one hand and covered his eyes.

"Evelyn?" my dad was saying. "Are you still with me? No, I don't want you. You had your chance, and you squandered it."

"Don't call me Evelyn," I said. "And yeah, I'm still here. I was just thinking."

"That was obvious. You never did have much of a poker face." He smirked. "I'll hand her over in return for the Damascene 'Scope."

"The Damascene 'Scope?" I repeated, surprised and relieved and afraid that I looked like Gideon had when I'd shown up on his doorstep. Even Dawkins looked surprised.

"You know what I'm talking about."

"The Damascene 'Scope," I said again, still processing. "Sure."

"And I want it to have three of those Verity Glasses in place so that it's functional."

Dawkins gave me a thumbs-up and wrote TELL HIM OK on a notepad.

"Okay," I said, then added, "but we're going to

need something in return."

"That's not how this works, Evelyn."

"Put Mrs. Sustermann on-camera."

"She's safe," he said. "I give you my word."

"I want to talk to her," I said.

"That is *not* going to happen, Evelyn." He breathed in and out a few times, something he always did when he was trying to control his temper. "You are *not* the one dictating terms here. She is safe. Even that foul cat of hers is safe."

The scratches on his face.

"Fine," I said, "so then show me the cat."

"Stop with this foolishness, Evelyn!" he snapped. "I am *not* going to show you the damn cat any more than I am going to show you a pink fluffy unicorn."

"That's because you don't have him, do you?" I said. "He probably got away."

"Why all this nonsense about a cat?"

"Because I don't believe you!" I almost shouted. "You lie all the time. Why should I take your word for *anything*?"

He did his phony chuckle—the one that meant there were things in the world I didn't understand and never would. "Evelyn, whether you believe me or not, I have Mrs. Sustermann, and if you'd like her back alive, you are going to bring me what I want."

Greta isn't the sort of girl who cries easily, but she turned away.

"Okay, okay," I said. I was all out of fight; now I just wanted to get moving on the next part, whatever it was.

"That wasn't so hard, was it?" Dad said, smiling. "Let's say we meet in Times Square in two hours, in that spot where we went that time. You pestered me for ages to take you to—"

"I remember," I said, cutting him off.

"Don't be late, don't forget the 'Scope, and don't bring anyone else, or we *will* kill Mrs. Sustermann." He winked. "*And* her cat. Bye, son."

He disconnected, and Dawkins pushed down the lid of the laptop.

"We don't *have* the Damascene 'Scope with us," Greta said.

"Doesn't matter," Dawkins said. "Even if we did, we wouldn't give it to the Bend Sinister." At the startled hurt on Greta's face, he rushed to add, "I don't mean we'd risk your mum's life, just that we'd find a way to dupe him *and* rescue your mum. We'll disguise some junk and tell him it's the 'Scope, and by the time he discovers it's not, we'll be far away."

"I'm not feeling so hot," Greta said, walking toward the back of the room. "I'll be on the bench in the ladies' room."

"She seems kind of upset with this plan," I said, once she'd disappeared into the back hallway.

"And why shouldn't she be? It's her mum's life in the balance." Dawkins looked over his shoulder at a dusty clock mounted on the wall. "He wants you there at eleven forty-five p.m. Times Square is going to be teeming with tourists."

"But it's a Monday," Sammy said.

"No matter the day or time," Dawkins said, "Times Square is *always* jam-packed."

"Big crowds are good, right?" I said. "Lots of people makes it difficult for them to nab me."

"And makes it difficult for us to nab *them*," Dawkins said. "But at least we'll be able to spot the Bend Sinister easily. With their business suits and blank-eyed stares, they'll stand out from the Times Square tourists. Thank goodness the meet wasn't on Wall Street."

"I really wish the rest of the Blood Guard were here," Sammy said, dropping back into his chair. He refreshed the Cat-o-Grapher screen. "They'd have our backs."

"Unfortunately," Dawkins said, "they won't arrive until early morning."

"Never mind them," said a voice. "You have *me*."

Diz was in the doorway, her beehive and lipstick perfect, looking like she'd just stepped out of a 1960s movie.

"Oh!" Dawkins yelped. He dashed across the room, threw his arms around her, and twirled her so that her feet left the ground. "You're okay! You're okay!" he cried. "I was worried!"

"Easy, champ!" she said, laughing. "You're going to tear the dress. Vintage Chanel doesn't come cheap!"

He slowed and set her back on her feet. "How did you get away?"

She swaggered over and set down her dinky purse and white angora sweater. "First, I stunned them senseless with one of my cab's 'Schlock and Awe' security features."

"The bright light and noise from the advertisement boards," I said. "We saw that from down the street."

"That knocked four of them out flat."

"And then you just sped out of there?" Dawkins asked.

"I would have, but one of their SUVs was following me, so I led them on a merry chase to Coney Island. That's where I lost them." To me and Sammy, she said, "Never try to outdrive a cabbie. We know all the short cuts."

"I really did fear the worst," Dawkins said.

"It's okay, honey," she said. "But why didn't you answer your phone?"

"We've been underground," Dawkins protested, and told her everything.

Diz sagged against the desk. "You *lost* her? After all that?"

"I'm afraid so," he said.

"Oh, Jack," Diz said. They walked off together, talking in low tones.

"You got an email," Sammy said, tipping his head toward the screen I'd used earlier. It was still logged on to ILZ. The inbox had a "1" next to it.

"Probably my dad changing the plan on us."

But when I opened my inbox, I found a message from Gideon.

To: DorkLord2K1
From: ArmaGide0n

No problem!!! It was weird and fun. But I think your game scared off the delivery person. Our pizza never came! I had to eat leftovers. Let me know if it's too late to join your ARG. I have a lot of friends on the boards and could probably put together a team of my own.

I must have made some kind of noise, because Sammy looked over and said, "You just squeaked. Like a little kid. You okay?"

"I'm *great*," I said, typing a reply. "My friend Gideon is okay."

"Oh, good," Sammy said. "He seemed like a nice guy."

And then, without consulting Dawkins or Sammy, I came up with a plan of my own.

Diz and Dawkins strolled back.

"Any change on the cat?" Dawkins asked Sammy.

"Nah. It's still sending a weird signal from the water by the Brooklyn Bridge."

"You say Greta went for a lie-down in the ladies' room?" Diz asked. She grabbed her clutch. "I'll go fix my makeup and see how she's doing."

Dawkins went to the one clean cabinet in the room and dug around inside until he came out with a green canvas duffel bag and some work gloves. He threw a pair to me. "Ronan, come out with me to the platform. There's some scrap on pallets in one of the storerooms— maybe there's something we can use to create a dummy 'Scope."

"I'll just stay here and watch the cat," Sammy said. "Because *that's* exciting."

We climbed the steps back into the fancy subway station. Immediately on escaping that dusty control room, I breathed easier.

We walked together toward the other end of the platform.

"He wants the Damascene 'Scope?" I asked.

"Probably knows we wouldn't hand over Greta and intends to follow you after the trade. And figures he may get something else he wants in the bargain."

The arches over the tracks began to glow with light.

"Train coming through," he said, pulling me into the shadows of the City Hall stairwell. "Unlikely anyone would notice us, but why risk it?"

A 6 train slowly followed the curving track around

and out the other side of the station. Once it was gone, we continued on our way.

"So what if you were right, what you said earlier, about the Damascene 'Scope being able to destroy souls. Are they going to destroy every one of the Pure souls on the planet?" I said. "That'd take forever. That can't be their plan."

"Even using the Eye of the Needle would take a long time," Dawkins mused. "They'd have to locate each of the Pure, defeat the team of Blood Guard protecting that person, use the Eye to comb out the soul, then stash the collected souls in a warehouse or wherever—somewhere, anyway, where the Grand Architect of the Blood Guard won't be able to perceive the trapped souls. You're right: it makes no sense."

"Something else that makes no sense: my dad burning down our house," I said. "It's been bothering me."

"Well that it might," Dawkins said. "After all, you were asleep upstairs."

"Not that part of it—I mean, *why* burn down the house? Because he was trying to make my mom expose the Pure she protected?"

"That's the Blood Guard's theory." Dawkins stopped walking.

"It's a crazy-dumb, desperate thing to do just to capture a single Pure—he'd be throwing away an under-cover identity he spent ages building." Years of playing the role of my dad, years of duping me into thinking he loved me and my mom. It had all been a lie. "But maybe that was worth the risk? Maybe once he had a single Pure soul, he wouldn't need to pretend anymore?"

Dawkins snapped his fingers. "That's why, the moment the Bend Sinister did capture a Pure, your father abandoned his cover and hit the road. Because it no longer mattered; he no longer *needed* the Pure your mum was guarding."

"Right," I said. "But why?"

"We have criminally underestimated the Bend Sinister," Dawkins said, walking again. "We'd been thinking they must collect as many Pure souls as possible, when all they really need is *one*."

"So then my dad gets Flavia's soul—mission accomplished, right? So why bring it to the Glass estate in that Conceptacle thing?"

"Because he thought he'd be able to permanently destroy it using the Damascene 'Scope," Dawkins said.

"What good is that?" I asked.

"I wish I knew," Dawkins said, heaving open a creaky metal door. On the other side were piles of gears and unidentifiable things all covered in rust and grease. Dawkins gestured at a fat, rusty section of pipe. "Voila—that lovely hunk of junk is going to be our Damascene 'Scope."

When we hauled our duffel back into the control room,

95

Sammy looked up. "The ping came aboveground and now it's moving up this street here."

"Maybe it's just the cat wandering around," I suggested.

"Some cat," Sammy said and whistled. "It can move at like fifteen miles an hour. And stops at intersections."

"That's Broadway," Diz said, tracing the street on the screen. "They're already heading to the meet at Times Square."

"How's Greta?" Dawkins asked.

Diz sighed. "Depressed, furious, hates *you*, and doesn't believe you're going to be successful in rescuing her mom."

"You know, a simple 'sad' would have sufficed."

"You asked," Diz said. She zoomed the map into the Times Square area. "Where is this trade supposed to take place?"

"Here," I said, tapping a triangle of pavement where Broadway crossed Forty-Fifth Street. "When I was six, my dad took me to see Mr. Met there—you know, the guy with a baseball for a head? He signed a jersey for me."

"I'm a Yankees girl, myself," Diz said. She sighed. "This is going to be a bear to stake out. Jack, you can maybe perch up here, on these benches by the TKTS booth, and I can wait over here."

Sammy stood up. "Don't forget me."

Dawkins guided him back into the chair. "You,

Sammy, will be our eyes and ears." He typed a few commands into one of the computers, and the live feed from the subway terminals changed to live feeds of Times Square.

"Whoa," Sammy said. "I didn't know you could do that."

"We're going to need someone to pinpoint Mrs. Sustermann's location using the cat's collar," Dawkins said.

"As well, you see anything scary going down, you warn us," Diz said.

"How am I supposed to warn you?" Sammy asked. "Telepathy?"

Diz rolled her eyes. "Using cell phones, of course."

"But our cell phones don't work down here," Dawkins said.

Diz laughed. "Of course they do, you idiot."

Dawkins held out his phone. "No bars, see?"

She took his phone from him and knocked it against his head, then tapped through a series of screens. "There is *wifi* here, Jack. Calls can be carried over wifi."

Sammy already had his phone out. "I don't see an available network."

"It's hidden," Diz said, then leaned down and logged him onto the network.

"Excellent," Sammy said. "So your plan is to leave me here alone?"

"No," Dawkins said, glancing back toward the

bathrooms. "Greta will be here. There is *no way* we are taking her to this meet-up with Ronan's dad. We have to keep her safe, for reasons you understand."

"Got it," Sammy said.

"Guys, this isn't going to work," I said. "I can't be talking into my phone when I'm going to meet my dad. He'll know something is up."

Diz carefully raised her chunky silver necklace over her head. "Here," she said, handing it to me.

"Thanks," I said. The necklace weighed a ton. "But . . . it's not my style?"

"It's against the law for taxi drivers to talk on the phone, so drivers use Bluetooth," Diz explained. "But that's way too obvious for a woman who wears her hair up, so I had a friend design a Bluetooth receiver that goes with my look. It's got a mic, little speakers, and—serious bonus—fashion value. Now, when people see me talking to myself, they just think I'm crazy."

I draped the necklace around my neck. "Right. *This* doesn't look weird at all. My dad won't think anything of my suddenly wearing jewelry."

"Say Greta asked you to give it to her mom so that she knows Greta is okay," Diz said. "That's exactly the sort of weird thing I would have done when I was a teenager."

"Okay," I said. "That will be my story."

"Now, Ronan, your task is to keep your dad occupied for as long as possible while Sammy uses the cat to pinpoint where Greta's mum is being held," Dawkins said. "Then Diz and I will go, grab her, and whisk her to safety. The moment she's in the clear, we'll tell Sammy, who will tell you, and you make a break for it."

"You think he'll just let me go?" I said. "He'll have people in the crowd."

"You'll have to evade them," Dawkins said. "You're trained, and you're smart, and they're going to be in dis-array after Diz and I take out the agents holding Greta's mum."

"This is hardly a plan at all," I said. "We should wait for the rest of the Blood Guard."

But Dawkins shook his head. "We can't risk that. I'm sorry, Ronan, but we have a very small window here. As long as your dad is operating by himself, we have a chance to best him and retrieve Mrs. Sustermann. But if he somehow rejoins the Bend Sinister, we will be vastly outnumbered."

Diz went to the restroom to fetch Greta, but came out looking scared for the first time since I'd met her.

She didn't have to say a thing.

In the little hallway to the restrooms was an open door. The words FIRE ESCAPE WERE PAINTED IN FAT RED LETTERS ACROSS IT.

"I swear, Jack, that door's been locked since the Nixon administration," Diz protested. "I know, because we've looked for the keys."

"Greta Sustermann doesn't need things like *keys*,"

Dawkins said, peering through the doorway. "Any idea where this leads?"

"To some metal stairs that lead up to a street grating," Diz said. She pulled on her sweater. "Should I go after her?"

"She'll be long gone," Dawkins said.

Sammy stood on the steps to the control room. "*This* door was sitting wide open. I bet she heard our whole plan."

Dawkins closed his eyes. He looked tired. "So we now have less than ninety minutes to catch Greta before your dad does."

"We'll take my cab," Diz said. "Let's grab our gear and bounce."

"What if we can't find her?" I asked.

"We *are* going to find her. I am not about to give up another Pure."

"*Another* Pure?" I asked. "You mean Flavia?"

"No, not Flavia. It was a long time ago—back in 1840," Dawkins said, leading us to the control room. "I'd been sent to Paris on my first solo assignment for the Blood Guard. The mission went south fast. I'll tell you all about it on our way to Times Square." He buckled on his sword belt. "And to be clear: I didn't *give up* anyone. But I lost her all the same."

CHAPTER 9
JACK DAWKINS, IMBECILE ABROAD

I was hungry, filthy, wobbly with exhaustion, and wearing a pair of scavenged brogues three sizes too large for my feet. After two weeks on the road, a run-in with four highwaymen, and an unfortunate encounter with a manure pile, I'd been left a beggar again.

I double- and triple-checked the address on the envelope.

Monsieur E. F. Vidocq, No. 13 Galerie Vivienne, 2nd arrondissement, Paris.

Galerie Vivienne was the sort of glass-roofed shopping arcade for the well-to-do that I'd only ever seen from the outside. The inside looked shady and cool, and a breeze blew that carried soft scents of chocolate and tobacco, perfume and flowers.

The walks were crowded with people. I didn't need a peek in their wallets to know they were wealthy—their clothes were a dead giveaway. The women's dresses were full of fussy, impractical bits that get in the way of real work; and the men's suits were too clean, too crisp, and fit too perfectly.

I didn't belong in this world.

A group of three women carrying parasols passed, glancing over and covering their noses with handkerchiefs.

They didn't think I belonged, either.

So, head held high, I marched right in.

Shoppers hurried out of my way and I reached number 13 quickly, then climbed the curving wooden staircase to the door above the gallery marked BUREAU OF UNIVERSAL INTELLIGENCE.

My knock was answered by a gruff "*Entrée!*" and I let myself into an office where a portly man with enormous graying sideburns sat writing at a rolltop desk. Even though some windows were open, the room was as warm and clammy as an armpit.

His eyes flicked at me, then he muttered, "*Les mendiants.* Be off if you know what's good for you."

"I have a letter," I said in my best French, which wasn't good at all. My mentor Jenks had given me a few lessons back in London, but I'd only just learned to read and write English; learning another language was beyond me.

The man held out his hand. "You'll get no tip from me."

Faint from hunger, I swayed on my feet and watched while he tore open the envelope and read through Jenks' note. I already knew what it said. She'd written of how I'd once been a petty thief and an orphan, but that she'd reformed me. She asked that Monsieur Vidocq train me for a month in the new art of "criminal detection." She'd signed the note "Love, M."

After he was done, he set the letter down and regarded me. "Mademoiselle Jenks believes that because I myself was once a thief and a convict, that I will have a . . . soft spot in my heart for you," he said in good English.

"Yes, sir," I said, relieved to be back in my native tongue. "She told me about your illustrious career with the police, how you founded the Sûreté, and now—"

"I have no taste for flattery," he snapped, waving his hand and then sniffing. "But I observe that you were robbed. And slept in a manure pile. And you took those shoes from a trash heap."

"I was pushed into the manure, monsieur, but everything else is correct! How did you know?"

"Observation. You come from far away yet carry nothing. Your trousers are stained along your thighs and backside from your fall. And those . . . *things* on your feet are so old that they are not worth repairing." He clucked his tongue and sighed. "Mademoiselle Jenks was correct. I do feel a tenderness toward you, Master Dawkins." He pronounced it *Dawkeen*. Turning back

103

to his desk, he grabbed a wooden-handled bell and rang it.

Immediately, a door opened across the room. A young woman my age glided in. She was willowy but looked strong like a dancer, and was dressed in close-fitting, simple black clothes. Her long blond hair was pulled back into a braid.

"Monsieur?" she said.

He flicked his fingers at me. "Mathilde, I am . . . we are taking on this new recruit."

Mathilde.

My target: a sixteen-year-old Pure who'd gone from starving street thief to private detective—and who was now in mortal danger. "Monsieur Vidocq is not one of us," Jenks had explained, "so he does not understand that his newest case involves the Bend Sinister. Our worry is that he has made this Pure girl a part of his investigation."

"Where are her usual Guard?" I'd asked.

"If any of that team joined Mathilde, she would become suspicious and have Monsieur Vidocq cast the person out. No," she'd said, "it has to be a stranger— you. But be careful: whatever diabolical business the Bend Sinister is conducting, hundreds of citizens have disappeared. Vidocq's team was hired to find two of the missing people."

Mathilde turned to me now, her eyes lit with obvious irritation.

"He will join you and Fabrice on the missing-persons case."

"*Oui*, monsieur," she said, bowing her head, "but he does not know your methods, and he is . . ." She fluttered her hands, exasperated.

"Nonetheless," Vidocq said, "you will train him. He will need new shoes, clothes, a bath, and . . ." He watched me sway in place. "How long has it been since your last meal, Master *Dawkeen*?"

"Catch me, please," I whispered, as my vision darkened and I fell toward Mathilde. I was aware just long enough to see her step aside as I slammed into the marble floor.

When I woke, I was on a cot in a dim room. There were three other cots, as well as open chests spilling clothes. A dormitory of some kind.

My head hurt something awful. Beside me, someone laid a cool, wet washcloth on my face, and I turned.

A young man with long brown hair and peach fuzz on his face smiled at me. Fabrice, I guessed.

"*Comment vas-tu?*" he asked. *How are you?*

In my pidgin French, I responded that I was well, thanks, and then pointed to my head.

He laughed and said in accented English. "You went down"—he smacked his palms together. "It was very . . . um, how do you say? Funny."

"I bet," I said, sitting up.

Somebody had bathed me and dressed me in black pants and a black shirt; folded over the foot of the cot was a white dress shirt and a coat. Beneath them were a pair of new leather shoes.

"Thank you," I said.

"It's nothing," Fabrice said, handing me a cutting board with meat, bread, and cheese. "Here, you will eat. We work tonight, yes? You must be strong!" He struck his right fist against his chest, clapped my shoulder, and left.

After the sun set, we made our way by streetlight and carriage lamp through the narrow alleys of the city. I'd been outfitted with four knives in secret pockets of my clothes, a stick of chalk, a pad, a pen, and a measuring tape.

I was completely lost within half an hour, which is when Mathilde clucked her tongue and said, "You, Englishman—you observe from here."

"What am I observing?" I asked.

Mathilde sneered. "Be quiet and learn! Fabrice will tell you." She stomped away into the darkness and around a corner.

Fabrice whispered, "She does not like you."

"I understood that," I said.

Fabrice explained that we were watching the entrances of the big glass foundry across the street, where during the day, teams of scientists and glass artisans made many of the best lenses in France. "They make big, as for lighthouses, and small, as for your eyes."

"What's that got to do with the missing couple?" I asked.

"*Je n'ais sais pas*." He shrugged. "That is what we will discover, no? They came here many times before they disappeared. So we observe. Mathilde and I, we must be in disguise, but you are perfect—the dumb English tourist who is lost and afraid." He drew an X on the wall by me. "If you leave, you make an O so we know. We will observe the other sides of the building and then come back for you in six hours."

"Six hours!" I said. "What time will that be?" I'd had a watch, but it had been stolen with my purse.

"Sunrise!" he said happily. And then he strolled off in the other direction, and I was alone.

Whatever happened in this district during the day, it must have been over by nightfall—there was no one on the streets. I found the shadowy doorway of a closed storefront, sat down, and cursed Jenks and Mathilde.

This mission was impossible. Sure, I could sit and watch this place all night every night, but that wasn't going to make Mathilde safe. In fact, for all I knew, she was on the other side of the building getting into trouble. The only way to keep her safe, I decided, was to wrap this case up as quickly as possible.

I watched the darkened windows until I'd almost

107

fallen asleep. There were no lights from inside, and no one went in or out, though a pair of rats did fight over something they found in a refuse pile in front of the building.

I chalked an O on the wall by the X, then drew out one of the needle-thin blades Vidocq had given me.

There was a long row of skylights along the roof. Maybe one of those could be unlocked.

Getting in was easy; the skylight locks broke with a few sharp hits. Getting down—*that* was the challenge.

It was only as I dangled from the window frame, swinging my legs back and forth, that I realized it was too dark to see anything below me. The building had no second floor; it was a straight drop down to the work-tables, kilns, and likely tons of glass breakables lurking in the shadows on the ground floor.

I'd need a rope.

I tried to raise myself back up, but I was still suffering from the four days without food, and all I managed to do was loosen my grip.

I hung there for another thirty seconds, feeling my hands cramp and weaken, knowing I couldn't hold on much longer.

So I let go.

I lucked out and landed on some kind of long work-bench.

But that's where my luck ran out.

I hit the edge, and the entire table flipped up, spilling me to the floor and catapulting everything on it into the air.

There couldn't have been that much on the table, but it sounded like I'd upended a barrow full of scrap metal on top of all the glassware ever made in the world. The crashing and smashing sounds went on for fifteen seconds, twenty, and then finally stopped.

I breathed as quietly as I could and listened.

Something else rolled in the dark, then fell and smashed.

The room was silent again.

"That wasn't so bad," I whispered to myself. Which was when I realized that I was now trapped in the center of a large, locked room surrounded by shards of broken glass that I couldn't see.

From now on, I told myself, *always carry matches.*

A quarter of an hour later, I noticed a thin sliver of light far off to my left: someone with a covered, shuttered lamp. I scooted behind the workbench I'd tipped over and waited.

I heard a man whisper something in French and recognized the word *Anglaise*—Englishman.

A woman's voice spat out an angry reply. I'd barely known her for a day, but already I recognized Mathilde's snarl.

I could hear their feet kicking glass.

"That was me, I'm afraid," I said in English, standing up.

"*Dawkeen?*" Fabrice asked.

"Over here," I said. "I thought I'd—um, see what was inside this factory."

"*Imbécile!*" Mathilde shouted. "Now they will know they are under suspicion!"

"If they're up to no good," I said, "then they already know. Uncover that lantern and let's see what they're hiding."

"What did you do? There is broken glass *everywhere*," Fabrice said.

There were a dozen long wooden tables, each filled with all sorts of tools and equipment. (Well, eleven—I'd knocked one of the tables onto its side.) There was a wall of kilns for glassblowing, and metal racks with dozens of molds for shaping molten glass.

"Look—all of these are molds of very ugly faces!" Fabrice said, holding one up. "Do they make masks in this place?"

One entire wall was taken up with wooden shelves, now mostly empty because my table had catapulted something right into the center support and all the shelves had collapsed. Unless something nefarious was hiding in the piles of shattered glasswork, there were no secrets in the workshop.

"Nothing!" Mathilde said.

"What about those doors there?" I said, pointing.

At the back of the building was a set of double doors with a chain looped through the handles.

We walked over and examined it. "There is no lock," Fabrice said.

"May as well see what's behind them," I said, unwinding the chain and then opening the doors.

"*Mon dieu*," Fabrice whispered, stumbling backward.

Mathilde stood frozen in place, her hands raised to protect herself.

I yelped and slammed the door closed, throwing my weight against it. "Run! I'll keep them here as long as I can!"

But no one pushed against the other side, so after a few deep breaths, we opened the doors again.

Inside was a long narrow room absolutely packed with people. They stood in rows eight or nine wide, and so deep that our light failed to reach the ones in the back. Hundreds of people, all of them standing still, staring straight ahead, their eyes open but dull.

"What *is* this evil?" Mathilde whispered.

CHAPTER 10

THE TRAP AT THE SPOT WHERE
WE WENT THAT TIME

"So what *were* all those people doing there?" I asked Dawkins as Diz's cab slowed along Forty-Fifth Street. "Were they zombies? Robots?"

"Zombies?" he repeated. "No, they weren't *zombies*, Ronan. But . . . a fuller explanation is going to have to wait until another time. We have arrived." He gestured toward a mob of people who'd spilled into the street and now surrounded the cab.

Times Square.

My family always avoided this place when we lived in Brooklyn, and looking around, I remembered why. There were throngs of people everywhere—families and foreigners and senior citizen tour groups; theatergoers wandering around in their fancy clothes, sailors in their dress whites, and street performers wearing everything from tuxedoes to Statue of Liberty costumes. It was nearly eleven at night, but the million chaser lights, neon signs, and billboards all over Times Square lit the streets up as bright as daytime.

"I *despise* this place," Diz muttered. She punched the horn, but no one seemed to notice.

"Sammy," I said, "can you hear me?"

"Loud and clear," came his voice from my collarbone.

"Any sign of the cat?" Dawkins asked.

Sammy sighed. "It is in a two-block radius of where you guys are now, but I can't pinpoint it any closer than that."

"Why not?" Dawkins asked.

"I don't know. Interference? The signal keeps leap-frogging between three—make that four—different sites. I mean, it's Cat-o-Grapher, guys, not some fancy GPS system. We're lucky it's *this* accurate."

Diz threw the cab into park. "This is where you get out, kiddo."

I looked out at the wedge of raised sidewalk where my dad and I had lined up for Mr. Met a million years ago. Bunches of people crossed back and forth, all of them looking up instead of where they were going. Standing in the center was a tattered six-foot-tall Elmo holding a sign that read PICTURES $20. Unbelievably, a couple of tourists in I ♥ NY T-shirts were haggling with him for a photograph.

"I have, what, a half hour until my dad shows up?"

"Yes. When we have Greta's mom, we will let you

know," Dawkins told me. "If we find Greta first, we will let you know. The moment both are safe, Ronan, you make a run for it."

"That's a lot to worry about," I said.

"So don't worry at all. Keep an eye out for Greta. And if she doesn't show, just focus on the meeting with your dad. Remember: stall him for as long as you can."

I popped open the door and immediately some guy in a tuxedo tried to get in.

"Hey!" Diz shouted. "Read the sign: I'm out of service!"

"I just need you to run me down to Canal Street—" the man said, trying to push past me.

"How about I run *you* into a canal?" Diz said.

The man backed off, and I slid out of the cab.

"Don't forget the 'Scope, Ronan," Dawkins said, as Diz popped the trunk.

I raised the hatchback and lifted out the duffel bag with the rusty pipe. A moment later, Diz goosed the engine, and the cab edged into the crowd.

I dragged the bag to the center of the triangle and triple-checked my phone's connection to the Bluetooth. "Sammy?" I said.

"Still here," he said. "And still mad about being left behind with the dusty ghosts of the subway."

"Sorry," I said. "You there, Jack?"

"Just getting into position, Ronan." I looked over my shoulder, where brightly lit red-and-white bleacher seats rose over the Times Square TKTS booth. "I'll be surveying the crowd from on high."

"Diz?" I said.

"Trying to stop myself from running over pedestrians," she said. "I'm heading down Forty-Fifth but will loop back around on Forty-Sixth."

And then, before I lost my nerve, I took out my phone, put Dawkins and Sammy on hold, and thumbed another phone number. "Everything is ready," I told the person on the other end when he answered. And then I merged all the calls.

"I don't know who you're talking to or what you got in that bag," said the giant photo-op Elmo, shaking a red fur finger at me, "but this is *my* spot, kid."

"Peace," I said, raising two spread fingers. "I'm just waiting for a friend." To be safe, I figured I should take a couple steps away from the guy.

"Live long and prosper, nerd!" Elmo said. "You nerds are out in force tonight, ain't you?"

I was tempted to correct him—two fingers in a V is the peace sign; four in a V is Spock's trademark—but I realized that would only confirm my nerd status. Somewhere in that crowd, my dad and his team of Bend Sinister agents were closing in. If I was going to get out of here alive, I needed to spot all of them before they spotted me. And, if I was lucky, before they even got here, I'd spot—

Greta.

"I see her," I said, as the crowd to my right parted for a moment. "She's under the marquee for *M: The Musical*. Still wearing her black hoodie."

"I'll head over and intercept her," Dawkins said. "Maybe I can tie her up and throw her in the cab."

"Hurry," I said. "She's coming my way. She's got to be *gone* before my dad gets here."

Greta strolled over with her hands sunk in the hoodie's pockets, then stepped up onto the concrete island and spun in place, looking out at the crowd. "Are you here by yourself, Ronan?"

"What do you think?" I said.

"I think that Diz and Sammy and Jack are probably all close by." She stared at my chest. "Why are you wearing Diz's necklace?"

"Long story," I said, grabbing her wrist. "Listen, we have to get you out of here right now."

Greta wrapped her fingers around *my* wrist and twisted her arm to throw me off balance, then yanked me over her foot.

I tripped and sprawled on the ground at Elmo's feet.

"What was *that* for?" I asked Greta.

"I'm not some maiden in distress to be carried out of harm's way, Evelyn Ronan Truelove," she said.

Elmo gave me a hand up.

"I never said you were!" I said, raising my hands in surrender.

"Then stop treating me that way!" Greta said,

shoving me. "I have just as much right to be here as you do. More, even, because she's my mom."

"But that's *exactly* why you shouldn't be here," I said. "You're not going to be able to think clearly. It's your *mom*."

"So I should trust you and Jack again?" She kicked the duffel bag. It clanked softly. "You think this thing is going to fool anyone?"

I looked down. "Not if they look closely at it," I said. "It's just to help buy us time."

"I thought we were friends," Greta said.

"We *are*," I insisted.

"It's obvious to me that you two care for each other," Elmo said.

"Hey!" I said. "This is private."

"Kid, you're doing this on *my* stage—oh, fine, I'll go over here." Elmo picked up his sign and wandered off to the far curb.

Greta took her hair out of her scrunchy, then pulled it back into another ponytail. "If you're really my friend, then you're going to do right by me."

I squinted up at the clock over Times Square: 11:31. Fourteen minutes until my dad was supposed to show. "The Bend Sinister are going to be here any minute now, Greta."

"It was you who got me mixed up in all this Blood Guard stuff, back on that train to DC. And you know what? I *trusted* you and went along with it." That wasn't exactly how things went down in my memory, but I didn't have time to argue. "But now they have my *mom*, Ronan. She doesn't know what's going on. She's probably terrified. So *we* need to fix this, you and me together. It's what friends do for each other."

She was completely right. True friends *are* there for each other, they *do* rely on each other, and they *should* have each other's backs no matter what ugly stuff the world may throw their way. "Okay."

"Okay?" she repeated, shocked. "Just like that?"

"You love your mom. I get it." I took her hand—not grabbing her wrist this time. "You *should* be here. But my dad said *just me*—not me and her daughter. If he sees you, it might ruin the deal."

She raised her other hand to her mouth. "Do you really think he'd flip out?"

"Who knows?" I said. "But why risk it? This is your *mom*."

"Oh gosh," she said, nodding. "I've got to go hide somewhere, so that I'm out of sight but close by if something goes wrong."

That was the best I could hope for. "Great!" I said. "But you need to go *now*."

"Too late for that, old boy," said Dawkins' voice. "I count . . . five joyless drones in ill-fitting suits on the north side of the square."

"You told me there wouldn't be that many," I said. "Does my dad have two teams?"

Greta stared at the necklace. "Jack?"

"Bluetooth enabled," I said. "Jack's back there."

Diz's voice came next. "Another two Bend Sinister suits on the west side making a beeline toward the center."

"There's too many for it to be just your dad's team," Dawkins said. "We've got company. Greta? Ronan? Abort this mission. It's not safe."

Sammy chimed in. "But guys—the cat's pings have stopped bouncing around! It's on the east side of Times Square, right between Forty-Fourth and Forty-Fifth Streets. Maps says it's in the atrium of the Grand Duchess Theater."

"That's just over there!" Greta pointed right.

"On my way," Dawkins said.

"I'll be behind you with the cab," Diz said.

Greta grinned. "My mom?"

"Ronan, Greta, don't wait for confirmation—just get out *now*."

"Okay," I said, and pulled Greta south.

Elmo called out after us, "Kid, your duffel bag!"

"I'll be back for it!" I shouted, weaving between a bunch of drunken college students and pausing at the curb. A slow stream of cars beeped along the street. "Soon as the light changes," I said to Greta, "we jog across and try to get lost in that crowd."

"Um, Ronan," she said, tugging on my shirt and pointing.

Facing us on the opposite curb were the three Bend Sinister agents from the subway: the bald, pizza-eating guy, and the two beautiful women. Pizza man waggled his fingers in a wave.

"What are *they* doing here?" I said.

"I don't want to know," Greta said, dragging me left. She shoved past one person after another, shouting, "Excuse me! Pardon me! Excuse me!"

But then we stopped short again.

Coming toward us were two dark-suited men wearing bowler hats. Part of my dad's team.

"North?" I suggested.

"North," Greta agreed, leading the way again, toward the red-and-white bleachers over the TKTS booth.

We passed Elmo, and he gave us a thumbs-up.

But our path was blocked by a line of tourists six deep watching a fire eater. We worked around the outside of the mob until I spotted a break in the crowd.

"This way," I said, squeezing through a gap between two people.

On the other side of them, the pavement was clear all the way to the next cross street.

"Now we run," I said.

But before we'd taken even three steps, a man in a pinstriped suit stepped into our path. His arms were held wide, and he had a smile on his face like he'd just found the one person he'd been looking for all his life.

"Evelyn!" my dad exclaimed, striding forward. "Such a pleasure to see you. And joy of joys, you brought your friend Greta with you."

CHAPTER 11
LEEROY JENKINS TO THE RESCUE

Beside me, Greta asked, "Do you have any weapons?"

"Do I *look* armed?" I said. "I left my sword in the duffel bag."

"No need to get snippy," Greta said. She looked around wildly. "We're *surrounded*, Ronan."

"Yeah," I replied. "By *friends*." And then I lifted my fists into the air and shouted, "LEEEROY JENKINNNNNS!"

My dad paused and looked behind him. "Evelyn?" he said, confused.

Greta asked, "Who's Leeroy Jen—"

A tinny voice trilled from the Bluetooth necklace around my neck: "LEEE-ROY JEN-KINNNNNS!"

Around us, Times Square erupted in cries of "Leeroy Jenkins!"—only a few people at first, but then dozens, and finally hundreds, shouting out the name again and

123

again, like some sort of weird geek war chant. In a few seconds, it had built into a roar that drowned out every other noise in the city.

Alarmed, my dad raised his hands and lunged.

But before he could close the distance, the space around him flooded with bodies—hundreds of people calling out "Lee-*roy* Jen-*kins*!" and pumping their fists in the air. The youngest looked to be about twelve, and the oldest were a bunch of leather-jacketed dudes in their fifties.

Suddenly we couldn't see my dad at all.

"What's going on?" Greta shouted.

"Tell you later!" I shouted back, holding the necklace up to my mouth. "Thanks, Gideon!"

"Been tracking you since you got out of that cab," came his voice from the Bluetooth. "Awesome turnout, am I right?"

Dawkins' voice cut in. "Ronan? Greta? An angry mob has taken over Times Square, and—"

"My friends!" I said. "Not a mob! Friends!"

"If you say so, Ronan," Dawkins said. "We have secured Greta's mum. We even have Grendel. Get out of there *now*."

Greta pressed her face against the necklace on my chest. "Thank you, Jack!"

"Where to?" I yelled, gently pushing her away. "Where should we meet you?"

"Diz's cab is in the breezeway of that theater."

Gideon's voice cut in. "Cops will break this up soon. Which way you want out?"

"East!" I shouted, and the word rippled across the crowd. "*Lee*-roy! *Jen*-kins! *East!* East! *East!* East!"

"Which direction is that?" Greta asked, trying to see over the heads of the people around us. "How are we supposed to be able to see—whoa!"

Suddenly hands grabbed us and lifted, raising us until we were bouncing above the crowd, bobbing on a sea of open palms.

For a moment I was terrified of falling . . . but then I realized these hands weren't going to drop us; they were all sharing our weight equally. It was almost fun. I relaxed and fell backward, and dozens of palms caught and cradled my back, head, arms, and legs, then floated me above the mob, rhythmically chanting "Lee-*roy*! Jen-*kins*! Lee-*roy*! Jen-*kins*!"

"*Ronaaaaaaaaaan!*" Greta screamed from over my right shoulder. "What's happening?"

"We're crowdsurfing!" I yelled. "Like at a concert! It's wild, right?"

"No! It's freaking me out!"

"Just let them carry you," I said. "They're friends."

It took five minutes for the crowd to pass us all the way to the ragged edge of the mob, but then dozens of hands closed around our limbs and carefully lowered us until our feet were on the asphalt.

I turned to thank the people who'd ferried us away

from my dad, but our rescuers had already turned their backs and rejoined the mob, still thrusting their fists in the air and shouting, "Lee-*roy* Jen-*kins*!"

"Who *is* Leeroy Jenkins?" Greta asked. "Should I know him?"

"It's a gamer joke," I told her. "Long, dumb story."

But Greta wasn't listening. Instead, she was craning her neck trying to see around the crowd. "Diz. Dawkins. My mom—where are they? He said east!"

"We got carried a little off course," I said. "The theater with the breezeway is down that way. Come on!"

We slipped along the fringe of the crowd until we spotted Diz's cab.

Or actually, the big flat screens attached to it.

They no longer showed advertisements for the Broadway musical *M*. Now they flashed a white-and-red warning to the crowd: BACK! AWAY!! NOW!!! Earsplitting *whuuuups* blared from beneath the hood.

But the crowd was too thick. People were packed in on three sides, and there was nowhere for the cab to go.

There was just enough room for me and Greta to slip in through the back door.

We pulled the door shut again, Diz hit a button, and the locks snapped into place.

Greta and her mom embraced each other, and Grendel the cat sat licking its paws between them and me, ignored.

"That worked out rather well!" Dawkins said from

the front seat. "Now if we could only find a way to clear this crowd out of our path."

"I've got that," I said. I held up the Bluetooth necklace and spoke into the mic. "Gideon? Our car is trapped at the Grand Duchess Theater! Can you get the crowd to open a path for us?"

Gideon unmuted his phone and all I could hear was the chanting of the ILZ flash mobbers. "I can try," he yelled. Then we heard him shouting, "Everyone go west! West! West!"

The crowd picked up the instruction, braided it into the Leeroy Jenkins chant, and passed it along. "*West! West! West!*" The wall of people around the cab surged left, away from the theater, until the way in front of the cab was clear.

"Props to you, Ronan." Diz goosed the gas and we began rolling south.

"Thanks," I told her, and sagged back into the seat next to the cat. "Hi, Grendel," I said, and held out my palm. He head-butted it, and I scrunched up the fur behind his neck until he purred so loudly I could hear it over the noise of the engine.

"I have no idea how you roped in hundreds of people to help us, Ronan," Dawkins said, "and I don't care: consider me impressed."

"It's all thanks to Gideon," I said, scratching the cat's ears. "He posted a call for help on ILZ and a couple dozen other gamer boards. Said we needed a flash mob in Times Square and gave the trigger phrase. I thought maybe a couple dozen people might show, but I guess the request went viral."

"They saved us," Greta said.

"We're not out of the woods just yet," Diz said, lightly tapping the horn.

Through the back window, I caught a glimpse of blurry shapes running after us. "We have company!" I shouted.

Three dark-suited figures leapt at the car—one landed on the roof, while the other two pulled at the doors. I recognized them: the bald Bend Sinister agent and his two partners, the dark-haired woman and the redhead.

"These three are annoyingly relentless," Dawkins muttered.

There was a sound of wrenching metal and then the rooftop flat screen flew out in front of the cab like a Frisbee. It bounced across the cement, glass shards flying everywhere.

"Hey!" Diz cried. "That's expensive hardware!"

Beside her, the redheaded woman drew back her arm and swung it hard at the driver's side window. Her hand bounced off the glass without even cracking it.

"Bulletproof!" Diz said, grinning at the redhead.

So the woman threw herself across the hood, wrapped her fingers under it, and tried to pull it up.

"Okay," Diz said. "That is quite enough."

She stabbed one of her pink-lacquered fingernails at the silver buttons on the dash, and a loud electric hum started under the hood. As the hum grew in intensity, Diz warned, "Everyone, make sure you're not touching any of the car's metal parts."

With a shower of sparks, the three Bend Sinister agents were flung away. The woman on the hood was thrown forward, the bald man backward, and the dark-haired woman bounced off the wall to our right. All three fell to the ground, rigid and twitching.

Beside me, Grendel suddenly stiffened. After a moment, he shivered and sat, looking around at all of us and blinking his big golden eyes.

"What did you just do?" Dawkins asked Diz.

"The chassis is wired to a high-voltage, high-ampere battery," Diz said. "Transforms the entire body of the cab into one enormous Taser—for moments like this, when I need to shock someone in a hurry."

"I'm afraid to ask what the third button does," Dawkins said.

"And I'm afraid to tell you," Diz replied.

The necklace around my neck buzzed, and Gideon's voice came through. "The police are here, Ronan, so everyone's taking off. Over and out!"

"Thanks, Gideon," I said, but he'd already hung up.

The mob at last behind us, we were cruising easily down Broadway and away from Times Square.

"That guy tore off my advertising board!" Diz muttered.

"The Guard will reimburse you," Dawkins said.

Diz looked sideways at him. "Ha."

"What? We reimburse people . . . sometimes."

"Are we really safe now?" Mrs. Sustermann asked, leaning against Greta. She looked exhausted.

"It appears so," Dawkins said. "I am sorry, Mrs. Sustermann, for the mishap on the subway, but I am very relieved to have you back with your daughter."

Next to me, the cat stretched and shivered, then pivoted its head around on its neck.

"For a while there, I thought we were goners," Greta said. "Escaping was almost *too* easy."

Grendel let out a long meow, then started hiccupping a series of screechy yips.

"What's wrong with Grendel?" Greta said, reaching over to pet him. "You okay, kitty?"

The cat quieted, then opened its jaws wide. "*Haaaaaa,*" it said. "Ha. *Ha!* HA." Its voice slid up and down the scale like it was trying out a new instrument. "Got away too easy? Whatever gave you *that* idea? Ha! Ha!"

CHAPTER 12
THE CAT'S IN THE BAG

"Grendel?" Greta said, leaning away.

The cat turned to her, bared its fangs, and made a *mwah-mwah-mwah!* sound halfway between a meow and a laugh. Then it crouched down and aimed itself at the back of Diz's head.

"Oh no you don't," I said, grabbing it by the scruff of its neck as it launched off the seat.

It snarled as I hoisted it up in the middle of the cab. "I will exact my revenge beginning with you, Evelyn Truelove!"

"Sure," I said, tightening my grip as it swiped at me with its claws.

"Your father cannot protect you now!" the cat said in its yowling singsong. "Not after I deliver all of you to Evangeline Birk!"

"He wouldn't help me, anyway," I said, trading a

131

look with Dawkins.

"Birk will name *me* the new Head!" screamed the cat.

"Oh my gosh, it's *you*," Dawkins said, his eyebrows rising. "The mysterious Hand who is too ashamed to show himself!"

So *that's* why the cat had gone all stiff and weird: the Hand had moved his consciousness into it.

The cat slitted its eyes. "I am *not* ashamed, soon-to-be-dead Blood Guard! I am stealth personified."

"Don't you mean 'catified'?" Dawkins asked.

"I can be anywhere! You cannot see me coming, because I am all around you."

"Yes, we've heard—you are legion and blah blah," Dawkins said, reaching forward and snapping the cat's jaws shut with his hand. "You really shouldn't talk so much. Spoils the effect."

The cat growled.

"So is *this* your particular gift from the Bend Sinister? You get to occupy mindless Bend drones and the occasional small-brained mammal? What a paltry talent."

He let go of the cat's jaw and it snarled, "Shut up! When Birk gets her hands on you—"

"She's going to have to find us first," Dawkins said. With his other hand, he unbuckled the cat collar and passed it to Greta. "Please throw that out the window. Diz, we need something in which to . . ."

"Under your seat," she said.

Dawkins pulled out a pink nylon gym bag, unzipped it, and held it open. "Ronan, just bung that little beast in here."

I held the cat inside the bag while Dawkins zipped it, releasing its neck at the last moment. The bag seemed to explode, the cat ricocheting around inside, looking for a way out and yowling.

Diz pulled over, and Dawkins marched the bag to the trunk, flung it in, and slammed it shut.

He got back in and smoothed his hair. "I'm sorry about your pet, Mrs. Sustermann," he told her. "But we couldn't have that beast see where we're headed."

I could still hear the cat howling and yammering in the trunk, but it was muffled enough now to be bearable.

Mrs. Sustermann stared over her shoulder out the back window. "That's all right. Whatever that was, it wasn't Grendel." She turned to Greta. "Honey, what is going on?"

"I'll tell you everything soon, Mom," Greta said. "I promise."

"Hello?" Sammy said via the Bluetooth necklace. "Remember me?"

"Hey, Sammy," I said. "Thanks for the help back there."

"No problem. I'm just glad you guys are headed back here. This place gives me the serious creeps."

"We're going to that moldy old subway station again?" Greta groaned.

"No," Dawkins said. "That's hardly secure. We're going back to the original plan: Agatha's penthouse at the Montana. We'll hide away in ridiculous comfort and await the rest of the Guard. And if the cat misbehaves, we'll feed it to the four Dobermans of the apocalypse."

"You'll do no such thing!" Greta snapped. "Grendel is probably still in there."

"Just kidding," Dawkins said. "Once we rid the cat of his Bend Sinister hitchhiker, Grendel will be back to his old self."

We'd been heading south toward downtown, but after a series of sharp turns, we were soon heading north up Madison Avenue. "We'll cut through Central Park and have you there in a jiffy," Diz said.

"You guys are *leaving* me here?" Sammy said. "That is stone cold."

"Just for a tiny bit longer," Diz promised. "I'll be coming for you right after I drop them off."

Except for the cat in the trunk, we were silent while Diz drove.

Then Dawkins said, "Mrs. Sustermann, can you tell us about the place you were held? Did you see the people who'd abducted you? How many were there?"

Greta's mom gave us a quick rundown of her abduction on the subway. She'd been blindfolded and then loaded onto a van.

"You could see it was a van?" Dawkins asked her.

"Not until about an hour later, when they stopped

134

and took off the blindfold," she said. "We were in this enormous room."

"Enormous as in stadium sized?" Dawkins asked.

"No, enormous as in *tall*—like fifty feet high," Mrs. Sustermann said. "The place was made from old brick. What I could see of it, anyway. There were wooden crates stacked like Jenga towers everywhere you looked. And carts full of electronic equipment."

"Such as what?" Dawkins asked.

"I'm not really a techie," Mrs. Sustermann said, shrugging, "so I couldn't tell you what I was looking at. I did recognize a defibrillator on a crash cart, though. That was strange."

About ten minutes after arriving, she explained, my dad came in through a pair of metal doors, complaining that someone he'd been expecting to meet wasn't there, but that it was just as well, since he wanted to make sure to deliver the right package.

"What was he talking about?" Mrs. Sustermann asked Dawkins. "What package?"

"It's something called the Damascene 'Scope." Greta winced and fiddled with her hands. "The explanation is complicated. But I swear that Dad will tell you everything."

"Greta is right, as usual," Dawkins said, facing forward so Greta couldn't see his face.

"Mr. Truelove is a— He's a bad person, Mom," Greta said.

135

Mrs. Sustermann laughed. "Oh, I've known *that* since he moved into the neighborhood." To me, she added, "Sorry, Ronan, but I never liked your father."

"It's okay," I said. "I don't like him, either."

Mrs. Sustermann reached out and squeezed my shoulder, then continued. "After that, he went on what he called 'an errand.' He left behind two men he said would kill me if I didn't behave."

"An errand," Dawkins mused.

At some point we'd taken Eighty-Fifth Street through Central Park. Now, as I watched, Diz turned the cab onto Central Park West.

"Whatever it was, it took him a couple hours. When he got back, his thugs zipped me back into the bag, loaded me into that van, and the next thing I knew, I was in Times Square and you two were cutting me out of it." She smiled at Diz in the rearview mirror. "Thank you, by the way."

Greta whispered, "I'm so sorry you had to go through all that, Mom."

"It's okay!" her mom said. "Most interesting thing to happen to me in months. And it was all worthwhile, because at the end of it, I got to be with you."

They said more to each other, and I tried not to eavesdrop, but it was hard not to hear, sitting next to them as I was. I should have been happy for them, but all I felt was sad. Greta didn't know it yet, but her family was ruined. Greta's dad was going to have to tell Mrs.

Sustermann the truth about Greta—the truth that Greta didn't know and could never be allowed to know, that she was one of thirty-six Pure souls in the world, and that an entire organization of people dreamed of killing her.

And because of that, Mrs. Sustermann would never be able to look at her daughter again without worrying, would never again trust that Greta was safe in the world. All Greta wanted from life was to have her family together, and she had the bad luck to be born a Pure.

It's not right.

"What's not right?" Greta asked.

"Huh?" I said, startled.

"You mumbled 'It's not right.' What are you talking about?"

I must have spoken my thought out loud. "Um, that my dad . . . He tried to break up your family. I feel bad about that."

She smiled at me. "But it didn't turn out how he planned. And now I get to have both my mom *and* my dad close by. So I should probably be *thanking* him."

"I wouldn't go *that* far, Greta," Dawkins called back. "But we can soon discuss this in comfort, for we have arrived." He grabbed his sword belt and climbed out. "I'll collect the beast."

The Montana was a huge century-old apartment building facing Central Park at Seventy-Second Street.

Thirteen or fourteen stories tall, it filled half a block, with tall peaked towers at each of its four corners.

With the squirming pink gym bag in his arms, Dawkins leaned back into the open window of the cab. "Give a call if things get weird," he said.

"Weird*er*, you mean," Diz said, putting the cab into gear and driving off.

"What time is it?" Mrs. Sustermann asked, yawning.

"Time to die!" the cat *mrowed* from within the bag.

Dawkins shook it hard. "You be quiet," he said, and checked his watch. "It's a quarter past midnight. A perfect time for us to sit down to a late dinner."

The front doors were unlocked, so we strolled right into the paneled entrance hall. A huge chandelier twinkled above us.

"Fancy!" Dawkins said. "But where's the doorman?"

On the desk facing the door was a well-worn laminated sign: BACK IN 10 MINS.

"I have Agatha's code," Dawkins said, "so we don't have to wait for this person to return from nature's call." He hit the call button and the elevator doors quietly slid aside on well-oiled gears. Dawkins tapped a code into the keypad for the south penthouse, and the doors whispered shut. After a moment I realized we were moving.

"Didn't think we'd ever actually get here," I said.

"Sorry about running away from the subway station," Greta said. "That wasn't so cool."

"It worked out okay in the end," I said.

"Mrs. Sustermann," Dawkins said, "there is much to tell you, and most of it will strain belief. But if you don't mind waiting just a while longer, your husband should be here in the morning, and he will be able to explain everything. Until then, we all need some rest, and I need a frighteningly large amount of food."

"As long as I'm with Greta," Mrs. Sustermann said, "I am happy to wait for the rest of the story. I'm sure it's a super cornnuts-cray—" She stopped midsentence.

With a soft *bong*, the elevator doors had opened onto a dark hall.

"Why is it so dark out there?" she asked.

"Hello darkness, my old friend!" the cat screeched.

Dawkins gave the bag a good shake and shoved it into Mrs. Sustermann's arms. "Keep that thing quiet, please."

In the light from the elevator, we could see a bit of the landing. Across from us, in front of a wall of green marble, was a long, narrow table with three enormous flowering plants in metal vases.

I felt a flicker of recognition. "Have we been here before?" I whispered.

"Not unless you're pals with a movie or TV star," Dawkins replied. He drew his sword.

"TV," I said. "That's it. This wall was behind my dad when he Skyped with us."

"Ah." Dawkins raised a finger to his lips and then tiptoed out into the hall.

I didn't have a weapon of my own, but I followed him out anyway, and grabbed one of the brass vases from the table. I dumped the dirt and big creepy plant onto the floor, then raised the vase over my shoulder, ready to throw.

At the entrance to the apartment, Dawkins gestured for me to go to one side of the doorway. He stood on the other. Then, with the toe of his sneaker, Dawkins gently pushed at the heavy mahogany door.

It swung open, onto a dark and silent apartment.

CHAPTER 13
WEAPONS OF BRASS DESTRUCTION

D awkins disappeared through the open doorway.
I wasn't sure whether to follow or not. All I
had was my ugly metal vase. But the first lesson Dawkins
taught me was that a Blood Guard finds weapons in
whatever he has at hand, so I gripped my ugly metal
vase tightly and stepped forward.

And then someone inside hit the lights.

There was a Bend Sinister agent fifteen feet in front
of me. I blinked at the sudden brightness, but I didn't
need to be able to see to fling the vase.

I scored a direct hit, and he fell backward over a
fancy red couch-bench thing. He kicked his legs in the
air and rolled to his feet, a bloody welt on his forehead
and fury in his eyes.

But by that time I'd grabbed a fat brass bowl from a
table by the entryway, and I hit him with that, too.

The third time he got up, I was ready with a metal sculpture of a very tall, very thin person. I swung it at him like a baseball bat and scored a home run: he slumped down onto the couch and stayed there.

"Nice work on the guy on the divan," Greta observed from the doorway.

"Greta!" I said, looking over my shoulder. She and her mom had come in, her mom holding the squirming pink gym bag. "It's not safe! We don't know how many there are." My foot squelched in something wet. I looked down: blood.

"There is no way I'm sitting out there like a damsel in distress," Greta said, pulling the door shut and locking it behind her. "I trained for the Blood Guard, too. Give me a weapon."

The knocked-out guy in the foyer had a sword. I dragged it away with my foot and slid it over to Greta. Then, getting a better grip on my statue–baseball bat, I followed the trail of blood around the corner into an enormous living room. There were two couches and a bunch of chairs around a fireplace, and in front of them was Dawkins, standing over a little muscly guy in a suit—clearly another Bend Sinister agent. The man was out cold.

Next to them, bunched up like a closed accordion, was a rug.

"I took out one of them in the other room," I said.

"And I pulled the rug out from under this fellow,"

he said, tapping the guy's chest with the point of his sword. He looked at me. "Please put down the priceless Modigliani, Ronan, and use this instead."

I set the sculpture down as he tossed the man's sword to me. I reached out and caught it by the hilt.

He smiled. "You're getting better at this. Now let's see if anyone else is lurking in the apartment."

I pointed to the black iron staircase that climbed up to a second floor. Dawkins shook his head. "This floor first." But the huge kitchen was empty, as were the media room, dining room, and bathrooms.

"He'll have taken Agatha," Dawkins said. "Judging from that trail of blood, the dogs did not go gently."

But when we came back into the living room, Agatha and three of the Dobermans were waiting with Greta and her mom. The fourth Doberman was lying on the couch, his torso wrapped in a bandage.

"Aren't you a joyous sight!" Dawkins cried. He picked Agatha up and hugged her, then turned his attention to each of the dogs. "What happened to Pestilence?"

"When Mr. Truelove and his three agents walked in, I whistled the Dobermans to me and ran for my panic room." She pointed to the wall beside the fireplace; part of it had pivoted away from the corner like a door. It was a foot thick and made of steel, with huge lock bolts like a bank vault's. Behind it was a bathroom-size room with an easy chair, a table, and four TV monitors. "All of the dogs obeyed except Pesty. He attacked one of the men—buying us enough time to open up the room and get inside. I called him again, and this time he ran to me, but as he did, another of the agents slashed him with a sword."

"Brave pup," Dawkins whispered, kneeling by the dog and stroking his muzzle.

"You are one lucky little girl," said Mrs. Sustermann. "Where are your parents?"

It took me a second to realize she was speaking to Agatha.

"It's a very long story," Agatha said, frowning. "Who are you?"

"This is my mom," Greta said.

"Ah! So you did find her." Agatha scratched Pestilence behind his ears. "I patched him up as best as I could; there's a first-aid kit in the panic room."

"But no telephone?" Dawkins asked.

"It hasn't been installed yet," Agatha said. "I only purchased this apartment six months ago, and the contractors haven't finished all the work." She looked up at the fireplace, and I spotted something I hadn't noticed at first: a small, dark glass hemisphere attached to the wall. "But the closed circuit cameras *are* connected, so I was able to watch and listen while Truelove strolled around whistling 'Mack the Knife.'"

"He does that," I said. My dad always whistled when he was thinking hard.

"It was *beyond* irritating," she said. "After he

checked out both floors, he came back here and stared up into the camera."

"But he left all this priceless artwork!" Mrs. Sustermann asked. "What in heaven's name was he looking for?"

"Us," I said. "He wants *us*."

"He explained that he wasn't after me," Agatha said, "but that he didn't mind that I was hiding in there, watching, because now there'd be an audience when he delivered his prize to Evangeline Birk."

"That's the name," Greta's mom said. "The same one Grendel used, the one Truelove mentioned."

"Does that mean she's coming *here*?" I asked. I couldn't help myself; I looked back over my shoulder like she might be there already. "We have to get out of here *now*."

The pink gym bag in Mrs. Sustermann's arms writhed. "The glorious one is on her way! There will be no escape for you—just give yourselves up!"

"Excuse me," Dawkins said, taking the bag. He took three steps forward and swung the bag like a bowling ball, releasing it at the last moment so that it slid across the floor. The cat yowled as it disappeared into the other room. "To give us all a bit of privacy."

"Poor Grendel," Greta said.

"Agatha, how many can fit into that panic room of yours?" Dawkins walked over toward it. "It looks very small."

"Maybe two or three people? But then I'd have to leave the Dobermans—"

"Mrs. Sustermann," Dawkins said, waving her over. "We are going to need you to stay with our friend Agatha here until help arrives."

"The child?" Mrs. Sustermann asked, stepping inside the panic room. "Greta and I are happy to watch over her."

Agatha carried Pestilence back into the room and sat down in the chair with him on her lap. The other three dogs obediently crowded in.

"You, Agatha, and the dogs will be safe in here until your husband and the rest of our friends arrive. Which will be *very* soon."

"But Greta—" Mrs. Sustermann said, stepping back out.

"Will be with me and Ronan," he said, blocking her. "We are very good at taking care of each other, but we'll only be able to do that if we know you are safe."

"Please, Mom. The three of us can get away, but not if you're with us. You'll be okay in here," Greta said, hugging Mrs. Sustermann again. "We'll just find somewhere to hide out until help arrives."

"I don't like this one bit," Mrs. Sustermann said. "I haven't liked *any* of tonight."

"I know," Greta said, her face still tucked into her mom's shoulder. "It's not going to be like this forever, I promise."

But it *was* going to be like this forever, wasn't it? I looked away.

"I don't understand what's going on, but, well—I trust you." She joined Agatha in the room, the dogs sitting around their legs. "This *is* cozy," she said.

And then Dawkins pushed the heavy door shut and held it while one bolt after another was turned. When he stepped away, you couldn't tell there was a seam in the wall at all.

The three of us headed for the front door.

"Sammy," I said into the Bluetooth necklace. "Did you catch all that?"

There was no response.

"Sammy? Are you still there?"

"He's probably in the cab with Diz," Greta said. "On his way here."

"Let's get out of this building," Dawkins said, "phone up Diz, and meet them on the street."

The pink gym bag had come to rest against the side of the unconscious man in the entryway.

Dawkins looked down at him and then the vase and brass bowl I'd used to knock him out. "You attacked him with home furnishings?"

"Someone told me a Blood Guard can make just about anything into a weapon," I said, shrugging.

"Obviously a wise and rakishly handsome someone," Dawkins replied, reaching for the door.

But before he grabbed it, the doorknob rotated.

The three of us stopped and stared.

The knob twisted all the way, and someone on the other side pushed. But Greta and her mom had turned the deadbolt, and the door didn't open.

"Could it be Sammy and Diz?" Greta whispered.

"They don't have the elevator code," Dawkins replied.

"Maybe whoever it is will give up and leave," I whispered.

Dawkins shook his head. "Let's just back away *very* quietly."

We'd taken two big steps when whoever was on the other side of the door started pounding on it, hard.

"Burn it down!" commanded a woman's voice.

She was answered from behind us.

From the gym bag.

"*In here!*" the cat shouted. "*The ones you seek are in here! Birrrrrrrrrrrrrrk!*"

CHAPTER 14
A SLIPPERY SLOPE

"Birk! Birk! Birk! Birk!" the cat shouted.

"Second floor!" Dawkins hissed, pointing his sword at the circular iron staircase. He hooked the gym bag with his free hand as we ran.

"Why bring it?" I asked.

"The cat knows too much—it might tell them where Agatha is hiding," Dawkins replied.

At the top of the stairs was a sitting room lined on three sides by tall slanted windows.

"That direction will be only bedrooms," Dawkins said when I started toward a back hallway. "We are going out *this* way." He went to the windows and opened a set of French doors, and a cold wind gusted into the room, whipping the gauzy curtains like streamers.

Agatha's apartment occupied the top two stories of the peaked south tower of the apartment building, and the balcony looked out over Central Park, a vast field of shadow with a few strings of lights crisscrossing it— roads and footpaths. Stretching out beneath the balcony was the steep slope of the tower roof, and then a drop to the street fourteen stories below.

"No escape this way," Greta said.

"Guess not," I said, looking over Greta's shoulder. I gripped the doorjamb so tightly my fingers hurt.

"Don't worry, Ronan," Dawkins said, stepping back inside. "I'm not going to throw you off the balcony."

He went left and threw open another set of French doors, then stepped out onto that balcony, and announced, "Perfect! Between this tower and the north tower is the flat rooftop of the apartment building. If we can get down there, we can descend the fire escape to the street, and then hide ourselves in that big park over yonder."

"How are we supposed to get down to that fire escape?" I asked. "We're up here, and it's way down there."

He didn't answer, just ducked in and grabbed the gym bag.

"Birk!" the cat coughed. "Birkity Birk Birk!"

Dawkins smiled. "It looks to be about a one-and-a-half-story drop from the tower eaves to the main rooftop. So we hop over the balcony railing, slide down the slates, catch ourselves at the edge, and then carefully climb down to the roof below."

I took a step backward into the room. "I don't like this plan."

"High time to get over this newfound fear of heights, Ronan." He raised up the pink gym bag. "The cat will test it first," he said, setting the bag on the slate roof tiles on the other side of the railing.

The bag slid away fast. At the bottom edge of the tower roof, it vanished; I could just barely hear the possessed cat's infuriated yowl.

"Looks safe enough to me," Dawkins said, taking Greta's hand. He reached back for mine, but I stepped away. "Ronan, come on!"

A sound carried up the stairs—of wood splintering, a door being kicked in, maybe; of death and destruction headed our way. I glanced back.

That was when Dawkins lunged, tucked his left shoulder into my gut, and lifted me.

"You said you weren't going to throw me out the window!"

"Shush," he said, swinging his right leg over the railing. "Obviously I was lying."

The wind was fiercer on this side of the tower, pushing at us as he brought his other leg over and stood on the wrong side of the balcony railing.

Over his shoulder, I could see back through the open balcony door into the apartment. No one had appeared at the top of the stairs yet. Maybe they hadn't actually managed to get through the front door. Maybe there was a place to hide in the tower itself. "It's not too late to go back inside."

"Greta? Take my hand," Dawkins said. "On three. One . . ."

She climbed the railing and stood next to us, her red hair whipping in the wind. She took his right hand with her left. "Sorry, Ronan."

"Two . . ."

"Why are you always *carrying* me?" I said as Dawkins hit *three* and the two of them hopped from the balcony onto the slate.

We went a lot faster than a cat in a gym bag.

Maybe it was the wind pushing us, or the sharp slant of the tower roof, or the greasy, slippery grime coating the slate tiles, but we *zoomed* away. I watched the bright windows of the balcony grow small behind us, like my dad's face in my dream.

"Too fast," I wheezed.

"We're going too fast!" Greta echoed.

"I'll slow us down," Dawkins said, kicking his legs to one side and turning facedown. In the process, I slipped off his shoulder, bounced hard on my back, then rolled right over him.

There are probably hundreds of things a person can do to stop himself when tumbling downhill, but I couldn't think of any of them. I just hyperventilated, squeezed my eyes shut, and waited to die.

And then Dawkins' hand hooked around my belt.

With a jerk, I stopped rolling. He yanked hard and turned me, and his other hand reached out and took mine.

"I've got you, Ronan!" he said. He was sliding face-first, and I was sliding feet-first, and somehow it was even worse than before.

"We're going to run out of roof!" I cried.

Suddenly a chimney pipe was there, a solid black bar in the darkness that I hadn't been able to see at all until Dawkins slammed into it with his shoulder. There was a loud *pop* and the groan of crumpling metal, but he held tight to Greta and me and slowed us both down.

"What was that popping noise?" Greta asked.

"Collarbone," Dawkins gasped.

I was still slowly sliding. "Thank you," I whispered. "You saved—"

And then: air. My feet and most of my legs left the roof.

"I'm going over the edge!" I yelled. But then I stopped, half on and half off the slate.

"Shh," Dawkins said. "We don't want to be so noisy that they look for us from up there. We'll just wait here quietly until it's safe."

My cheek pressed against the dirty slate, I fixed my eyes on the balcony. It was well lit and faraway. From that vantage, we'd be just a dark smudge on the darker rooftop. They probably wouldn't see us.

But that didn't matter. Our friends were going to arrive at any moment.

"We have to keep going," I said, hating having to say it but knowing I'd hate myself more if I didn't. "We have to get down and warn Diz and Sammy."

Dawkins made a pained noise and said, "Right. Okay. You two starfish—spread your limbs and really hug the rooftop like you love it as much as a giant pizza."

Greta slowly moved her arms and legs apart and then let go of his hand. She didn't slide at all. "I'm good."

"Hey, I'm kind of dangling here," I said. "If I wiggle around too much, the weight of my legs will probably drag me right over."

"That's not going to happen—I've got you," Dawkins said. "Try swishing each of your legs around and see if you can find anything with your feet."

I closed my eyes, took a deep breath, and started slowly swinging my right leg back and forth, until I was able to raise it all the way up onto—

"There's a rain gutter," I said. "It runs along the edge of the roof."

"That's too flimsy to hold our weight," Dawkins said. "Try searching under it. Can you find a drainpipe? Old building like this, it will probably be a massive heavy thing."

I swept my right foot along the bottom edge of the gutter one way—nothing—then brought it up again and used my left foot to sweep the other side. I hit something hard.

"There's something over here," I said. "Under Greta. Maybe it's a drain pipe."

"Okay, here's the plan," Dawkins said, wriggling. "Ronan, I am going to pull you all the way up onto the slate. And then I am going to shimmy down that drainpipe to the roof below. After that, I'll guide each of you down, and if you fall, I'll be there to catch you."

"*That's* your plan?" I asked.

Without answering, Dawkins strained and dragged my whole body up until my feet stopped kicking air and only hard slate was beneath my toes. "Do the starfish, Ronan."

I spread my arms and legs wide and pressed myself against the roof.

"You can let go now," I told him.

"Ronan," he said, "I released you a minute ago. You just didn't notice."

Dawkins scooched past on his belly. "It's right where you said it was, Ronan. But I don't think we need it—there's an enormous air conditioning unit tucked up against the tower, so the drop's really not bad at all—maybe twelve feet."

He rolled over the edge. The sound of something heavy striking metal came up to us from below.

A heartbeat later, he coughed and said, "That was easy! Come on, you two. I promise I'll catch you."

"You going to be able to do this?" Greta asked me.

"Absolutely," I said, breathing deep. "Or, you know, *probably*."

"Okay," she said, pushing off. She used the gutter to carefully lower herself. "It's like gymnastics," she said. "You were a gymnast, right?" And then she disappeared over the edge.

Dawkins grunted. "Your turn now, Ronan."

I copied Greta, using the gutter to slow myself, then eased my body down and let go.

Dawkins caught me and fell back onto his butt. "Nicely done, you two," he said. "Now to warn our friends."

The air conditioner unit was as big as an RV, and like an RV, it had ladder handholds built in. Getting down to the tar paper–covered expanse of the roof was a cinch.

A long, sad meow came from a dozen feet away.

Dawkins went to the gym bag, unzipped it, and took out Grendel. "That insane Hand appears to have vacated this poor cat. Sorry about the rough treatment, puss," he said, scratching its head. He gently put it back into the bag. "We'll get you someplace safe and give you a nice plate of tuna."

Greta shook her cell phone. "Sammy's not answering! Why isn't he answering?" She stabbed at the screen and said, "I'm going to try my dad."

"My mom," I said. "They're coming here, too, right? We need to warn them."

"All in good time," Dawkins said, leading the way to the fire escape. "First we must get safely down to the street."

Greta went first, her feet ringing on the metal ladder.

I was about to climb after her when I heard a shout from behind us and the sound of something heavy smacking the rooftop.

A Bend Sinister agent, dazed from having slid down the slate roof and right off the edge.

Dawkins ran over and swung his sword hilt-first against the man's temple. "One down! Let's not dally and run up the score. Ronan, the fire escape!"

"Wait," I said, pointing at the street. "Look!"

On the sidewalk, a familiar cab was parked at the curb, right behind two white vans. Based on the pink hair, the person next to the cab had to be Diz, and the person beside her was probably Sammy. Facing them was a group of ten people I was overjoyed to see: the Blood Guard. Greta's dad was down there, and so was my mom.

"About time," Dawkins said. "Let's hurry down and join them."

But before I'd reached even the first landing of the fire escape, everyone had already gone inside. I took out my phone and tried Sammy again. This time, he answered.

"Ronan!" His voice came from the chunky silver necklace I was still wearing under my shirt. "Everyone's here—we're on our way up to Agatha's now. Had to hotwire the elevator, because the doorman's missing."

"There are Bend Sinister agents all over the apartment!" I dropped my phone back into my pocket and kept talking while following Greta down the rusty stairs. "The Guard needs to be prepared for a fight."

Sammy said something, and I heard a voice I happily recognized as Ogabe's say, "Is that so?" And then an alarm rang.

"Okay, we stopped the elevator," Sammy said. "We're getting out on the floor below Agatha's and taking the stairs." Someone said something, and then Sammy said, "Fine, okay! Everyone else is going to the apartment. But I'm supposed to take the elevator back down, because I get left out of everything. Where are you guys?"

"On the fire escape at the front of the building," I said. "We had to get out in a hurry. But let them know Agatha and Greta's mom are still inside, in a safe room on the first floor."

We heard him tell everything to the rest of the Guard, and then he got back on the phone. "Okay, your mom says to be careful. I'm coming down. See you guys in a couple minutes."

We'd reached the final landing, and Dawkins carefully walked out along the final narrow metal staircase until its counterweight rose and it tipped down to the ground. Greta went after him, and I came last.

I fell to my knees on the sidewalk. It was

wonderfully solid.

"No call for melodrama, Ronan," Dawkins said, pulling me to my feet. "It wasn't *that* high up."

Greta took Grendel out of the bag and kissed his head. "Sorry, little man! But everything's okay now." He *mrowed* in confusion, but seemed happy enough to be in Greta's arms.

"Maybe we should go in and help?" I asked, thinking about my mom. "We don't know how many Bend Sinister agents are inside."

"I can tell you how many of us are *outside*," said a woman's voice. "Six."

She stepped out from between the white vans. She was small, dark haired, and wearing a well-tailored suit. "I am Legion," she said.

And then her voice-but-not-her-voice came from our left, from the mouth of a huge guy with white hair. He had a Tesla gun aimed directly at Greta's heart. "I am the one who is many."

Greta dropped Grendel and held her hands up in the air.

Beside the huge guy was the dark-haired woman from the subway platform and Times Square. She had a sword pointed straight at my eye. "I speak through all," she said.

From behind us came two more Bend Sinister agents, both armed. The bald guy who'd been eating the pizza slice held a Tesla gun inches away from Dawkins' head,

159

while the redheaded woman touched a blade to his chest. "Defy me and you defy an army of millions!" said the redhead.

"*Millions* is a bit rich, isn't it?" Dawkins said.

A black panel van pulled alongside us on the street.

"Get in," said the small woman.

The redheaded woman and the bald man took our weapons, while the huge white-haired man pulled our arms behind our backs and fastened them with thin plastic strips—zip ties, Diz had called them.

The woman spoke again. "Miss Birk will escape the Blood Guard, as she always has. In the meantime, I will take you three someplace where we can get to know each other a bit better."

"Sounds ducky," Dawkins said.

The bald guy slid open the side door of the van, and we were shoved face-first onto the floor. The huge guy grabbed our legs, rolled us the rest of the way inside, and then climbed in after, followed by his three fellow agents.

Last was the redheaded woman. She paused to pull the door shut.

Before she did, I glimpsed Sammy step out onto the sidewalk. He looked around, confused, then bent down to pet Grendel. A moment later, the cell phone in my pocket thrummed.

But by then the door was closed and we were rolling away.

CHAPTER 15
ZIP TIE MEETS ZIPPO

"Where are you taking us?" I asked, hoping that Sammy could hear even though the Bluetooth necklace was between my chest and the dirty floor of the van.

"You'll find out soon enough," said the small dark-haired woman—the Hand who called herself Legion. "Three, collect their cell phones."

While Bald Pizza Eater patted down our pockets and took our phones, the exotic-looking woman zip-tied our feet.

The bald agent handed the phones to Legion, and I watched as she dropped them into a silver Mylar envelope.

"Faraday bag," she said, smiling so that dimples appeared in her cheeks. "Blocks signals so that no one can use these pesky things to track us. Now where's my cat?"

"Grendel?" Greta asked, rolling her shoulders to try to get a hand out of the zip tie. "We left him back there."

"You left him *behind*?" Legion said, angry. "First you put him into that terrible bag, and now you leave him alone on the streets of New York? What kind of monsters are you?"

"The bag was for *you*," Dawkins said. "To stop you from seeing where we were."

"Oh, I know," Legion said, "but though I could see nothing from inside the bag, I *heard* plenty. Once Birk arrived, all I had to do was exit the cat and return to my body, then call her team to learn your location. After that, it was a simple matter to show up and capture you for her."

"That doesn't sound simple at all," Dawkins said.

"And if you're capturing us for her, then why are you driving us *away* from her?" I asked.

"You three are far too valuable a prize," Legion said. "Miss Birk will return to the site of the Reckoning, and then I will deliver you."

"We're a *prize*?" Greta said. "That's . . . weird."

"Former Head Truelove thinks you three are valuable for some reason," Legion said, "so we're going to take a closer look at you. And if one of you truly *is* special, you'll have a role in the Reckoning."

"Ooh, that sounds important," Dawkins said,

glancing at me. "What is it, some kind of black-tie party?"

Legion's smiled flattened. The bald agent drew back his leg and kicked Dawkins in the head.

"I don't appreciate your tone," Legion said.

"Few do," Dawkins said, wincing.

"Will my dad be there?" I asked.

Legion rocked back in her seat, squeaking out high-pitched laughter. "Your dad? No. Your dad imperiled our entire project. He had the prize, and he let it slip through his fingers. *And* he failed to secure the Damascene 'Scope." She stopped laughing abruptly. "Where is it, by the way?"

"I expect it's a mound of slag in the furnace of a steel foundry by now," Dawkins said.

"We feared the Guard would do something drastic like that," Legion said. "Which is why we continued with the other option."

"Ah," Dawkins said, "is this that Reckoning shindig you mentioned a moment ago?"

The bald man kicked him again.

"Be quiet," Legion said.

After a series of looping turns, the van idled while the driver got out and opened some creaky metal doors. When he climbed back in and drove us forward, the darkness outside the windows changed: it went from night sky lit by streetlamps to bare brick walls.

We came to a halt and the Hand's agents clambered out, then reached in and lifted out each of us like a stick of wood. They carried us to a flat dolly as big as a queen-size bed and laid us on it faceup—Greta, me, then Dawkins. The huge guy got behind the dolly and followed Legion and the rest of her team, steering us down a ramp into a big old room.

Or I guess it'd be more accurate to say it was *tall*. The walls were made of red brick and rose up fifty or sixty feet. Most every inch of floor space was filled by teetering stacks of crates piled four or five high; coils of cable, mounds of metal rods, cardboard cartons, and tons of other junk. A mountain of giant plastic-wrapped spools teetered in one corner.

A single flood lamp dangled from the ceiling, throwing a harsh light on everything and filling the empty spaces with shadows.

This had to be the place my dad had taken Mrs. Sustermann. But if he'd been thrown out of the Bend Sinister, why would he show up at one of its strongholds?

"I like what you've done with the place!" Dawkins said.

Legion walked back to the cart. "Keep talking. There *are* fates worse than death, you know. What would happen if we just weighted you down and threw you, a Blood Guard Overseer, into the river? You'd sit on the riverbed for years—decades! centuries!—unable to move, unable to die, unable to live."

"I do love a good bath," Dawkins said. "So we're near a river?"

Legion reached into Dawkins' shirt and yanked out his Verity Glass. "I'll keep this, if you don't mind." Then she did the same to me, pausing only to lift the chunky silver necklace off my chest. "What's this?"

"All the kids are wearing them," I said. "In school, I mean."

"Fashion," she said with disgust. She let it drop back, then searched Greta. "Why doesn't this girl have a Verity Glass?"

"My mom," Greta said quickly. "I was using it to prove to her that the Blood Guard are real, and she still has it."

Legion clucked her tongue. "You need to be more careful with your valuables!" Turning to us, she said, "Tell you what: I'll keep the girl close by." She motioned, and two agents—the bald one she called Three and the exotic woman—picked up Greta and carried her over to a metal chair. "Anything strange happens, one of my team will carve her up with a sword. How does that sound?"

"Sounds pretty mean," I said. "I hate to hear what you have planned for *us*."

"Oh, nothing fancy. You two will be cooling your heels in a cell until Miss Birk returns." She waved her hand over her head, and the huge guy wheeled us through an archway and up a ramp into a hallway. He

165

parked the cart beside an open metal door to our left. Then he picked up Dawkins and heaved him into the dark.

There was a sound of something heavy falling over, and Dawkins shouted out in pain.

The huge guy turned to grab me next, but I'd already sat up. "I can totally get in there by myself," I told him. "Save you the trouble! It's no problem!" I swung my feet to the floor, stood, then hopped around him and through the doorway.

He slammed the door behind me, turned a key, and left.

I couldn't see a thing in the lightless room. "Jack?" I asked. "Are you okay?"

"No," Dawkins said, sounding pained. "He threw me on top of a big pile of rusty somethings, and they fell over on top of me."

"Sorry." And then, hoping that somehow the Bluetooth could still talk to the phone, I said, "Sammy?"

"Why are you calling for Sammy?" he asked. "He's not here."

"I've still got Diz's Bluetooth necklace."

"Ah! Sure."

From the dark in front of me, I could hear a squeaking noise. "What is that noise? Are there rats in here?"

"The noise is *me*. Some of these rusted things are sharp. I'm using one to saw through the plastic of the zip ties."

"This is the place my dad took Mrs. Sustermann, isn't it?" I asked. "But if he was thrown out of the Bend Sinister, why turn up here?"

"Maybe he went to deliver his prize only to discover once arrived that he'd nabbed the wrong person."

There was a *snap*, some rustling, and then Dawkins struck a flame from his Zippo lighter. "Tell you what," he said. "You stay by the door. I'm going to burn off the ties around my feet and then come and free you."

He bent over double, his body obscuring the flame. "Hot hot *hot*," he said. "Did they have to put those things on so *tightly*? Nearly set my pants on fire."

Holding the lighter aloft, he picked his way across the floor. "Sheesh. So much junk in this place."

"Where are we?" I asked as he crouched down behind me. I could feel the heat of the flame on the insides of my wrists.

"Pull your arms apart, Ronan. And . . . there."

I snapped my arms up and flung the melted remains of the zip tie away.

"Now for your feet." He kneeled down.

"Ah! Ah! Ah!" A moment later, the heat disappeared, and I was free.

"Sorry! Just a tiny bit of singeing on your ankles!" He stood and raised the flame high so we could see the whole of the room. It was a concrete bunker with an arched ceiling, filled with giant rusted pulleys, forty or fifty cardboard boxes marked RATIONS, and crates marked POTABLE WATER.

Dawkins reached inside one of the rations boxes and pulled out a dented can. "Lima beans. Yuck. But at least we have water." He took out what looked like a gas can, uncapped it, and took a big gulp. "Hmm . . . tastes like tin."

"Looks like the door is the only exit," I said, picking up a nail from the floor.

Dawkins inspected the stone around the steel door with the light from his Zippo. "The hinges and bolts are on the other side. And the frame of this door is solid steel. But this place was never meant to be a dungeon, so that old lock likely isn't supersecure."

I got on my knees and squinted into the keyhole. "Maybe I can use this to pick it." I showed him the nail. Back at Wilson Peak, Greta's dad had given us weeks of training in lockpicking, but the only A student had been Greta. "I'm going to need something to use as a tension wrench."

Dawkins swept his hand across the floor and offered me a thin, flat strip of metal—a band that had been around a crate at one time. "Will this work?"

"Maybe," I said, and wiggled the metal strip and nail into the keyhole. "This might take a while. I'm no Greta."

He slumped down against the door, the Zippo cupped in his hand, while I scraped the nail around in the lock, feeling the mechanism and saying nothing. Finally I asked, "So what *were* all those hypnotized people doing in that glassworks?"

"I'd really rather not finish that story," Dawkins said. But he almost immediately relented. "We had no idea what we'd stumbled upon, so we did what kids always do when they get into deep water: we asked an adult for help."

CHAPTER 16

A FOUNTAIN OF STARS

Monsieur Vidocq did not believe us at first.

"Hundreds of dead bodies, you say?" he asked the morning after our discovery, scratching at the thick fur of his sideburns.

"Not dead, but alive. They breathe," Fabrice said. "Their chests rise and fall."

"Alive but they do not mind you three going through their pockets?" He dropped his hand on the stack of documents we'd taken from the people in the room. Very few had actual identification papers, but many had receipts or calling cards or bank vouchers with scrawled names.

"They were mesmerized," I said. "Under some sort of spell."

He narrowed his eyes at me. "A *spell*."

"The couple we are searching for," Mathilde said,

unfolding one particular sheet. "They are among these people."

She handed him a bill of delivery for a Mme Adrien, with her address and signature.

"It was in the pocket of her dress," Mathilde said. "See? She signed for it on the day of her disappearance."

"And her husband?" Vidocq asked, peering at the bill.

"Beside her." Before he could ask how she knew, Mathilde added, "They wear matching wedding rings."

Vidocq patted the documents again, and then took a clean sheet of paper out of a drawer. He dipped his pen in ink and began copying names. "If this preposterous story is true," he told us as he wrote, "it will be easy enough to find these people among the rolls of the missing in the offices of the Sûreté."

I'd been there only two days, and already I'd fulfilled my mission. The policemen of the Sûreté would confirm the missing persons, Mathilde would be safe again, and I could go home to London.

"There was no one in that room," Vidocq told us the next day, sitting down at our table.

The names *had* belonged to the missing, so he and his policemen friends from the Sûreté raided the glass-works while we waited at a café.

"But they were there!" Mathilde insisted.

"Perhaps," Vidocq said, signaling the waiter, "but

they are there no longer. The room held only piles of broken glass." He raised an eyebrow. "Apparently some vandals broke in a few nights ago and destroyed three months' work."

"So that's it?" I asked. "A dead end?"

"Not quite," Vidocq said, sipping at his espresso. "As we sat discussing the allegations against their workshop, I observed an employment notice on the wall."

I took a swallow of my coffee—

"They are looking for a girl for their front office," he said.

—and spewed it all over the table.

Fabrice used his napkin to wipe it up. "You are wasting good coffee!"

I ignored him. "You don't mean to send Mathilde into that place!"

"That is precisely what I intend," Vidocq said. "Unlike you, she is able to live by her wits."

"But it's . . . dangerous," I protested. Instead of merely observing this glassworks, Mathilde would be working there. I hadn't completed my mission at all. I'd only made things that much worse.

"All of a sudden you are all white and slimy, like *blancmange*," Fabrice said. "Three days and already he is in love!"

"*Imbécile*," Mathilde said, standing up. She flipped her blond braid over her shoulder. "Monsieur Vidocq, I will go prepare." She gathered her coat and left.

"I am *not* in love with her," I insisted to Fabrice and Vidocq. "I barely know her!"

They laughed, because they understood what I did not: that I was lying—to them, and to myself.

Mathilde wasn't at the office when we returned.

As we climbed the stairs to the door, a slouching peasant girl in a shapeless gray dress crossed the landing with a message. Her dirty brown hair hid her face to such a degree that when I went to give her a sous for her trouble, she couldn't even see my hand.

"Mademoiselle," I said. "For you."

"*Dawkeen*," she said, raising her face. "You are *such* a blind fool."

She wasn't wrong.

Vidocq clapped, delighted, and said, "We shall christen you *Sophie*!"

He brought in a forger friend to create documents, paid a clerk he knew to add an entry to the city's registry of births, and couriered money and instructions to a couple in Montmartre to play the parts of parents should anyone come round their muddy hovel asking about a girl named Sophie.

A few days later, Sophie won the position in the glassworks. The plan was for her to observe the goings-on from within, take notes, and then to hide her notes in the day's trash, which was collected each night by a removal cart.

"That is where you two come in," Vidocq told us. "You are to be shovel boys!"

Ours would be filthy, backbreaking work. Removal cart teams labored from dusk to dawn and smelled like what they hauled—mostly the horse manure that city sweepers left piled at the sides of the roads.

"He is punishing us," Fabrice told me that first night, "because *you* dared to woo Mathilde!"

"I have *not* wooed Mathilde!" I insisted. "I don't even know *how* to woo Mathilde. Now what does the note say?"

We'd found it curled inside the hollow handle of a trash bin, as per the plan. It was written in code, which Fabrice knew well enough to decipher.

In the afternoons the clientele of the glassworks changes. The new visitors do not purchase any wares; instead, the Burques show off what one glassblower calls the fiery furnace—*a kiln as big as a room, used only for "the special project." What is that? He will not tell me.*

"This is interesting, but it is not about the missing people," Fabrice said.

"We don't know that yet," I told him. "We don't know anything."

"I can testify to that," said our cart driver, another agent of Vidocq's. "Because if you did, you'd know we have to get a move on if we're to finish our work by dawn."

The next week's note was about the fiery furnace itself.

The glassblower swears the only things fired in the furnace are people. They die? I asked, alarmed. No, he said, they "volunteer, sweat inside all night, then come out alive, but like . . ." He let his jaw drop and his eyes glaze over. "Empty-headed cows!" He laughed. But why? His answer is mystifying. "Each person infuses one small blob of glass for M. Burque's grand mask." But what mask that is, I do not yet know.

I'd known something awful was under way—the hundreds of hypnotized people in the back room had been proof of that much. But this fiery furnace that cooked people? For some kind of mask?

"You must pull her out of there," I told Vidocq.

"You must mind your place," he said, skimming her most recent report. "It is not for *you* to tell *me* what to do. Mathilde is safe, and she is looking for the evidence we need to arrest this Monsieur and Madame Burque."

The next night's note was the most alarming yet.

I spied on the evening shift. A client was shown out of the fiery furnace, and then a demitasse of molten glass

176

was removed: the "infused" blob. It was blown up into
a whisper-thin glowing sphere that, in the darkness of
the glassworks, appeared to have a face—a visage like a
demon that moved *inside it. The tissue-thin bubble was*
forced into a mold, the mold dunked in water, and put
on a rack to cool. Stenciled #334.

There was nothing I could say to convince Vidocq to
cancel Mathilde's mission, so it fell to me. I'd have to go
in the next day, destroy her cover, and force the owners
to fire her.

"When I see that dumb expression of yours"—
Fabrice furrowed his brow and pooched out his lips—"I
know it means you have a stupid idea in your head."

"I don't have ideas!" I insisted. "I'm just thinking
about . . . our work."

"Even I know you're lying, boy," said the cart driver,
cracking his whip. "But if it's work you're pondering,
why not get back to it?"

It was dawn by the time we'd emptied our load at
the dump. I threw my shovel into the cart knowing it
was my last shift ever. Then I went to my bed in Vidocq's
back office and prepared.

The glassworks was closed and locked up when I arrived
at two that afternoon.

I walked around the building, banging on
doors until at last a window opened, and an older,

elegant-looking woman told me to go away.

"I am here for a friend," I said. "Sophie? I am . . . her fiancé, Jacques."

The woman smiled and said, "I am afraid to disappoint you, Jacques, but Sophie has been given the afternoon off. She probably awaits you at her boarding house. *Au revoir!*"

She closed the window and I stood staring at it for a long minute. This wasn't going according to plan.

I was trying to figure out what to do next when I heard a faint hiss. But though I looked all around, I couldn't place it. A second hiss thoroughly confused me. I prayed no one was watching as I spun circles in the middle of the street.

And then I was hit in the head by a stone.

It knocked me to the ground. When I reached back, my fingers came away bloody. "*Ow*," I said, looking around one more time.

Finally, I looked up.

Mathilde's furious face stared down at me. I didn't need to be any closer to hear her whispered, "*Imbécile!*"

When I joined her on the roof, she immediately started hitting me.

"Easy!" I said. "They might hear you!"

"They will not," she said. "It is far too noisy down below. What are you doing banging on the door and asking for me?"

"Something terrible is going to happen," I told her. "And I don't want you to get hurt."

"You are like a loyal puppy. Sweet, but dumb." On her belly, she edged forward so that she could just peek through the skylight. I joined her. "This is the moment," she said. "They are removing all the masks, you see?"

Below us, the worktables had been cleared, and now lined up across their tops were faint rows of nearly invisible glass faces. Hundreds.

"What are they going to do with them?" I asked.

"I think we shall see, no?" Reaching down between us, she took my hand and squeezed it.

For hours we watched, unobserved, as workers in aprons and gloves gently sandwiched pairs of the glass faces together, heated them until they melded, and then repeated the process. By the time the sun set, they had combined all of the faces into one very solid looking mask. It had a bloodred cast to it.

"What are they adding to it now?" Mathilde asked.

One of the workers kept touching it with a rod of white-hot glass, then pulling the rod away so that it trailed a thin strand.

"Hair," I said. "He's giving it glass hair."

When at last he had finished, the man took the mask to a vat of water and lowered it. A cloud of steam enveloped him.

When he emerged, he was holding the mask in his hands. He walked over to an older couple—

"The Burques?" I asked.

"Mmm hmm," Mathilde said.

—kneeled down, and held it out to them. The wife gestured to her husband, and he raised it to his face and put it on.

Mathilde gasped. "Is it *eating* him?"

The mask *moved*, squirming around on his face like it was alive.

"No," I said. The man didn't seem hurt. He had raised his arms in the air with what looked like exultation. "It's just . . . changing shape somehow."

Every second, the mask rippled, and every second, another face rose up from its folds of glassy flesh as though out of liquid. Plump faces became gaunt, sharp noses broadened, large eyes shrank under heavy brows. A whole population of faces passed through the mask's features.

"It's all of them," Mathilde whispered. "The missing people. They are *in* that thing somehow. That's why their bodies were in the storeroom; they didn't need them anymore."

Below, the man lowered his arms, and with his right hand, he touched his temple. Slowly, the forehead of the mask split open and revealed a third eye. It glowed an absinthe green.

"What is *that*?" Mathilde asked, kneeling and pressing her hands to the skylight for a closer look.

"We've seen enough," I said. "Let's go get Monsieur Vidocq."

I stood as the man below looked at his hand through the mask, waved it around as though it cast a shadow, and then turned and looked back, straight at Mathilde. There was absolutely no way he could see us in the dark—I was sure of it.

And yet he did.

He pointed and shouted something that we could not hear.

Startled, Mathilde leaped to her feet, lost her balance, and fell.

Right through the plate glass of the skylight.

I reached forward and tried to catch her, grabbing the back of her old gray dress, but all I managed to do was tear it and pull myself after her.

She had the good fortune to land in the vat of water where the glassmakers cooled their work. Me, I wasn't so lucky.

When I came to, I was bound to a wooden chair on top of one of the worktables. I was bleeding from dozens of little cuts, and my left arm dangled uselessly from my shoulder like an empty sleeve; I guessed I had some broken bones. Mathilde, completely soaked and indignant, was bound to a chair atop a table across the aisle from me.

"Who are you, Jacques—if that is even your name?"

asked the woman who'd sent me away earlier—Madame Burque. She spoke in flawless English. "Our Sophie won't tell us why she is here, and she does not understand *what* she is, but I'm betting you do." She was beautiful, this Madame Burque. She looked like a kind person as she came close, laid a hand on my cheek, and asked me, "Are you with the Blood Guard?"

"No . . . whatever that is," I said.

"You're a poor liar, Jacques." She smiled. "But I *thank* you. We did not know if our mask, *le percepteur*, would work as we'd hoped. But now we do."

She picked the red mask up. Off her husband's head, it had stopped squirming. "Until now, the Bend Sinister had no way to see the light of the Pure." She raised it up. "Every person in the world can sense the faintest glimmer of the Pures among them. They don't know what it is that makes them like or trust that Pure soul, but just under the realm of the conscious mind, they see the aura nevertheless. We distilled that ability—distilled people's very souls, the thing in them that responds to the Pure—and we combined them. Together, those hundreds of souls are able to perceive what the naked eye of a single person cannot."

"Bully for you," I said. My left arm was useless, but I had almost managed to slip my right from the ropes.

She laughed and took a thin rod of white-hot glass from a kiln. "You *are* one of the Guard. It is a pity you

182

won't be able to tell your friends of our success. My husband was confused to see his shadow when he put on the mask. Until he looked up and saw that *she* was the light source!" With a pair of tongs, she drew the end of the glass rod forward so that it formed a long thin point. And then she dunked it in water. "And now, for the second part of our experiment!"

"What's that?" I asked, my right arm free.

"Why, the killing of a Pure, of course!" She used the tongs to snap off the blobby tip of the glass rod. What remained was razor sharp. "Her first, and then you."

"*Dawkeen?*" Mathilde called out. "What is she talking about?"

"Don't!" I shouted, rocking the chair back and forth. "It's not—"

But Madame Burque only turned and hefted up the glass rod like a spear.

"Close your eyes!" I shouted in French, and Mathilde did, just as Madame Burque thrust the spear of glass through her heart.

Mathilde strained against the ropes holding her, coughed, and then slumped forward and began to die.

I cried and lunged at Madame Burque, but all I managed to do was knock my chair off the worktable and to the concrete floor. I landed on my broken arm, and the pain nearly overwhelmed me, but I kept my eyes open, and that's how I saw it: a stream of sparks geysering up from Mathilde's body.

"The stars!" Madame Burque whispered. "So beautiful!"

She, her husband, and their two workers stared in wonder as a silent stream of light made of thousands of bright motes flowed from Mathilde's body, a wondrous column of sparkles that rose straight through the skylights and up into the night, where it split apart like the blazing branches of a burning tree, speckled lines of light shooting off in dozens of directions.

It was the most beautiful thing I have ever seen in my life.

And also the most horrible.

And then Mathilde's head rolled back on her neck and a pulse of energy blasted out from her. It wasn't a sound, a light, or a wind—but somehow all three at once.

I was fortunate in that I'd already fallen to the floor and rolled under a worktable. Everyone else in the room was struck fully by the departure of Mathilde's soul.

Madame Burque and her husband were slammed into the wall behind me; the glassworkers were blown in the other direction. Every piece of glass in the building was pulverized.

After a few minutes, I realized that my chair had broken when I fell; I could work myself free. I stood, and looked at the devastation around me. It was as though an explosion had gone off. The Burques and their assistants appeared to be as dead as Mathilde in her chair in front of me.

It was difficult to see the knots through my tears, but after some time, I managed to untie her. Then I cradled Mathilde in my arms and carried her home.

Chapter 17
Borderline Crazy

"She was *dead*?" I asked. "For real?"

"Yes, Ronan, *for real*—and it was a disaster in many ways. The premature death of a Pure always has repercussions—natural and manmade disasters I don't care to enumerate. Mathilde's death was no exception."

"That's . . . terrible," I said.

"Yes, yes it was," Dawkins said. "It was the first and only time I saw the blazing bridge some Blood Guard have written about. Each of the thirty-six Pure are linked, and when one of them dies, the other thirty-five *feel* it."

"Feel what?"

He shrugged. "Who knows? A tickle of electricity? A wave of sadness? A sense of a light having gone out in the world? Whatever they feel, it's the passing of a Pure soul that causes it."

I leaned my head against the grimy door and said, "I'm really sorry, Jack."

"Thanks, Ronan," he said. "Was a long time ago, but your sympathy means a lot, anyway." He reached over and tapped the lock. "Get back to work."

"Did someone at least find the people from the glass-works?" I asked.

"No. The bodies were never found—not the hundreds of people who'd sacrificed their souls for the Perceptor, not the workers who'd fashioned that evil mask, and not the Burques."

Something in the lock cylinder gave, and the nail in my hand moved freely. Gripping the flat metal band, I wiggled both and carefully twisted them.

The lock gave out a high-pitched creak.

Eyebrows raised, Dawkins reached up and tried the handle.

It turned.

"Bravo, Ronan!" he said, standing and giving me a hand up.

"Thank you, Greta, you mean," I said. "She's the one who showed me how."

"No, I meant thank you, Ronan," he said. "It was you who did it."

We eased the door open and stuck our heads around the corner. The flatbed dolly was still parked outside, next to a row of crates that lined the hallway all the way into the big room.

"I don't see anyone," I whispered.

"Me neither," Dawkins said. "Let's see if we can't find a better vantage."

We kept to the shadows behind the row of crates and crept forward until we could see into the big main room.

A small metal hatch had been raised in the wall opposite the main doors, letting in a fiery orange light. We could see Legion, her team of Bend Sinister agents, and on one side, tied to a chair and forgotten, Greta. Standing by her, a drawn saber at the ready, was the huge guy who'd locked us inside the bunker.

"Those cartons piled beside Greta," Dawkins said. "I can use them to sneak up close to her. But if I simply charge in, that big dolt with the sword will act before I am able to rescue her."

"You're going to need a distraction," I said.

"A really *huge* distraction," Dawkins said. "Something foolish and noisy. Something borderline crazy."

I couldn't stop myself from grinning a little bit. "What did you have in mind?"

He eyeballed the dolly parked by our cell. "You played baseball, right? How good's your pitching arm?"

The dolly wouldn't budge.

While I kept watch, Dawkins had stacked the old ration cartons from the bunker onto the dolly in the shape of a big U. "You'll coast down into the room on this dolly," he'd explained, "safe behind these walls of cartons."

"Safe?" I'd repeated.

"*Relatively* safe, for a minute or two," he said. "You'll want to flee the dolly and hide once it's reached the far side of the room." He picked up a fifty-year-old pint can of pasteurized milk. "This was the closest thing I could find to a baseball's weight and size. As you coast through the room, lob these at that big flood lamp."

"They'll see me," I said.

"Obviously, Ronan," Dawkins said. "That's what 'distraction' means. Anyway, if we're lucky, you will smash the bulb, and we'll have a few sweet minutes of darkness to rescue Greta and get out of this place."

It wasn't the greatest of schemes, but we didn't have a lot to work with, and we didn't have a lot of time. So I gave Dawkins a thumbs-up and said, "I'm good to go," and then watched as he slipped down the passage and vanished around the corner.

It was only after he was gone that I discovered the dolly was too overloaded to move.

I tried again, leaning against the push bar and straining until my sneakers slid backward.

Soon Dawkins would be in position, counting on me to create a distraction. There was no way around it: I'd just have to remove a row of cartons from the wall he'd built up. Less cover for me, but maybe I'd be going fast enough that it wouldn't matter.

I went around to grab a box off the front, and that was when I spotted the black canvas pull strap, almost invisible under the front edge of the cartons. The strap had been tightened against the base of the dolly, but when I tugged on the buckle, it spilled out a loop big enough for me to fit loosely around my waist. I could drag the dolly like an ox with a cart.

I stepped into the loop, raised it to belt height, and leaned forward.

The dolly rocked slightly on its wheels.

I tried again, this time throwing all my weight into it.

The dolly rolled an inch and then stopped dead.

I lunged against the strap again and again, until the dolly had some momentum and was rolling along without stopping.

Pulling the dolly got easier fast. Pretty soon I didn't have to lunge anymore and was almost jogging, the strap tight around my waist, the dolly gaining speed right behind me as it neared the ramp at the end of the hallway. I had it going at a nice clip when a thought hit me: the dolly was going to accelerate on the ramp down into the big room.

And *I* was in its way.

I tried slowing down, but the wall of boxes on the front of the dolly nudged my shoulders.

I had no choice but to pick up my pace.

Of course, that meant the dolly picked up its pace, too.

By the time I hit the ramp, I was flat-out running for my life, the speeding dolly right on my heels. Knocking out the light was no longer an option, since I couldn't reach the cans on the dolly. But somehow I still had to draw attention away from Greta and Dawkins.

So I did what came naturally.

"Help! Help! Help!" I screamed. "I can't stop it!"

Did they turn and watch? Come after me with their swords in hand? I had no idea. I was afraid to look, afraid I'd trip and be run down.

Instead, my dolly and I hit the floor at the foot of the ramp and kept going—straight at two towers of crates next to the wall fifty feet ahead of me.

I had maybe three seconds before I would be smooshed like a bug.

When I'd crossed half that distance, I glimpsed a line of shadow between the two crate stacks: a narrow space.

I started tugging left, steering toward that gap.

In response, the dolly slewed the other way, pulling me right.

But by then I had run out of floor.

I leaped into the opening, and close on my heels, the dolly chewed through the wood, spilling cartons and packing material in its wake.

Luckily, the crates were stacked three deep, and the dolly stopped before it made it through the second row.

I fell between the third row of crates and lay there for a minute, out of breath and gasping. A single pint of condensed milk rolled away from the dolly and against my foot.

Greta.

I was supposed to have busted that flood lamp. Grabbing the can, I crawled out of the canvas pull strap and stood up.

That was when the stacks—already rocking back and forth because of the damage from the cart—started to fall over.

The gap I was standing in was too narrow for anything to hit me, but I could hear crates falling and splintering and breaking in the room. Along with people shouting. Probably at me.

There was just enough space between the back of the crates and the wall for a skinny thirteen-year-old, so I slid between them and worked my way out.

When I did, I found an open gray metal fuse box on the wall in front of me.

I ran my hand down the breakers and shut off each one.

"Lights out," I whispered, and plunged the room into darkness.

Apparently, none of the Bend Sinister agents had flashlights. Or maybe they couldn't find them in the sudden dark.

I made my way forward, crouched, and peeked around the spilled mountain of crates. Against the orange light from the open hatchway, I could make out three silhouettes.

"Two! Four!" Legion shouted. "You go after the girl and the Overseer. Five and Three, come with me. We'll make sure the Truelove boy didn't survive his little accident."

The silhouettes strode toward where I was hiding.

"I hope you're not hurt too badly, Evelyn Truelove," Legion called. "Speak up so that we can dig you out from this mess."

No way was I going to open my big mouth, but if it was noise she was looking for . . . I gripped the can of condensed milk.

Then, winding my arm, I hurled the can back to where the dolly had crashed. The can made a satisfying series of thumps and rattles as it bounced around in the wreckage.

"We hear you, Evelyn," Legion said, changing course. "There will be no escape, you know. Evangeline Birk is on her way, and with her will come many of my brethren—too many to hide from."

I jogged across the room and ducked behind the cartons Dawkins had used to sneak up on Greta.

And plowed right into someone.

A hand covered my mouth.

"It's us," Dawkins whispered. "That was inspired!"

Greta was crouched next to him, holding a sword. "That was *insane*," she whispered.

"Two? Four?" Legion said, sounding alarmed. "I can't reach you—what's happened?"

Dawkins gestured: two Bend Sinister agents were out cold on the floor. "That ruckus you made covered a *lot*," he said, handing me a sword and sword belt. "You'll need these if we're going to get out the front door."

A loud buzzer rang.

"An alarm?" I asked, buckling on my weapon.

"I doubt it," Dawkins whispered. "Otherwise it would have gone off a long time ago."

"She has arrived!" Legion cried. "You won't be able to hide from twenty of us, Blood Guard."

"We need another way out," Dawkins whispered. "And fast."

"Five, Three, throw wide the doors and welcome in Evangeline Birk and her army of true believers. The time of the Reckoning is upon us!"

CHAPTER 18
THE BLAZING BRIDGE

The room flooded with bright light as three black vans drove in. Dark-suited Bend Sinister agents poured out of the vehicles, twenty of them at least. Last of all, a towering, pale, white-haired woman in fancy red-and-gold robes emerged.

She stopped to speak with someone—probably Legion—then the white-haired woman stepped in front of the headlights and held one hand high. All the agents got down on one knee.

"Three of our enemies are here, hiding in the dark. Find them and bring them into the light." She clapped. "Go."

"Evangeline Birk," Dawkins whispered. "We meet again."

"Again?" I asked.

"That way," he said, pointing. "We'll be briefly

visible as we pass through that open hatchway, but it's our only option."

We'd taken cover behind a pile of crates twenty-five feet from the hatchway. Lying on its back in the orange light from the hatch was the metal chair Greta had been tied to, cut zip ties scattered around it.

"Jack," I said. "The chair."

"A bit too utilitarian for my tastes," he said. "What about it?"

"*Throw it*," I said. "Use it as a distraction."

"Good idea." Dawkins nodded. "The sound will draw their attention for a hot second, but then they'll glance back the other way. So the *moment* you hear the chair hit, you run."

"I'm ready," Greta whispered, crouching down like a sprinter.

"Me too." I faced forward.

Dawkins burst out, dropping and sliding the last ten feet flat on his back. He caught the chair with one arm and hugged it to his chest as he shot all the way across the floor to the far wall.

Then he rolled to his feet, took the chair by its back, and spun around like a hammer thrower. Once, and then faster a second time, and the third time so fast that he seemed to blur. After the fourth spin, he started generating wind.

When he slowed down abruptly, the chair had vanished.

He'd hurled it.

It struck a faraway wall and *gonged*. Then it must have ricocheted into something else, because for a good minute, things banged and rang and cracked and tumbled.

But by that time we were long gone.

The hatchway opened into a low, narrow tunnel with fiery orange cloth walls. We sprinted along single file, Greta, then me, and then Dawkins. We had to run stooped over and step carefully—the tan metal floor was little more than a foot across and curved at the sides, with fat riveted seams every eight feet. "Where *are* we?" I whispered.

"No idea, but we're climbing," Dawkins said at the same moment I realized we were going uphill. "Happily, the slope of this tunnel has hidden us from the view of anyone who takes a peek into that open hatchway back there."

"Guys," Greta said, "Krisco, that artist who wrapped up the Brooklyn Bridge—that's *this*!"

And I remembered the ride across the bridge, the cab filled with orange light.

"This beige metal beneath our feet? It's one of the main cables. These two wires holding up the orange ceiling? They're called auxiliary cables. We should probably use them as handholds. And it's so bright in here because of all the lights on the bridge."

"So that building we just left was the . . . anchorage,"

Dawkins said, "the place where these giant cables are fixed to the ground with tons of steel and concrete. Which explains those big spools back there—the silk for this Krisco fellow."

Greta thumped her hand against the soft fabric wall. "We're inside that stupid art project."

"I thought you said it was a cool art project," I asked, feeling queasy.

"Cool earlier, but stupid now that we're stuck in it with the Bend Sinister chasing us."

The main cable under my feet felt as solid as the ground, and thanks to the silk around us, I never really had to think about how high we were climbing. I just ran my hands along the auxiliary cables on either side of us and followed Greta. The uphill slope wasn't so bad, and the seams every eight feet made good footholds.

We climbed fast and in silence.

And maybe it was because deep down I was a little bit terrified, or because I had a Pure in front of me, that Dawkins' story of the death of Mathilde still rattled around in my brain.

Even if we managed to get Greta out of here safely, what would happen next? Sooner or later, my dad would tell the Bend Sinister what he'd figured out, and then Greta would forever be a target. She and her parents would have to start all over again, always looking over their shoulders for some random Bend Sinister nutcase who'd recognize Greta and attack her. And then Greta would suffer some sort of awful death like Mathilde.

It was no way to live. That wasn't the kind of life I would wish on even the meanest kid at school, let alone my best friend.

That was when I noticed the slope of the cable was getting steeper.

"We're at the tower!" Greta called back, and at about the same time, I came out of the silky tunnel into the blustery night. Next to me, loose ends of fabric snapped and billowed in the wind, casting flickering shapes on the orange-wrapped wall in front of me. The shadows almost made it look like the tower was on fire.

"*Great*," I said. As if this whole escape could get any more like my nightmare.

The wrapping ended right before the place in the front of the tower where the suspension cable disappeared into the brick. But the tower was swaddled in orange silk, too.

For the first time, I could see how high up we were.

A hundred feet down, six lanes of cars sped in both directions, and a hundred and fifty feet below that, the waters of the East River glinted in the moonlight.

"Ronan!" Dawkins shouted from behind me. "You *must* keep going."

"I can't," I said, feeling my knees lock and my stomach drop like in my dream of my dad.

"We can go over the top and down the other side!" Greta shouted.

"Listen, friend," Dawkins said. "Just turn your face forward, and you'll see a ladder not a dozen feet away. And once you're there, you're safe as houses."

I did as he told me and saw Greta clinging to the rungs, waving at me and shouting, "Come *on*!"

I thought again about the life she had before her. Someone had to help save Greta from that. And who better than me?

I got moving again, and before I knew it, I'd reached the caged ladder that snaked from the cable up to the roof of the tower.

"I'll be right behind you," Dawkins said.

There was nothing left to do but climb.

I was shocked when, moments later, I reached the top. The tower roof wasn't nearly as big as I'd always imagined—thirty feet across at the narrow points, and maybe a hundred feet wide. A metal railing crisscrossed the center of it. That and the flagpole at the center were the only things that were *not* wrapped in silk.

I crawled the fifteen feet from the edge to the center railing, the fabric weirdly soft and springy under my hands and knees. Then I rolled onto my back. I'd expected to see stars overhead, but the sky was overcast, and all I saw were dark storm clouds.

After a moment, Greta and Dawkins came and stood over me. They stared left, toward the center of the tower.

"What's all that for?" Greta asked.

I pulled myself up and turned to see what she was talking about.

Fifty feet away, in the center of the tower roof, was a flagpole, the Stars and Stripes snapping in the wind at its top. Piled near its foot were things I hadn't noticed during my crawl to the railing: carts of electronic equipment—monitors and things that looked like they belonged in a hospital. And encircling the flagpole was a spiky forest of steel rods, sixty or eighty of the things, all sticking straight up eight feet or more. They were in concentric circles and connected by wires to a silver metal rectangle in the center that looked like a bed frame standing on end.

"I don't know," Dawkins said. "But whatever it is, it can't be good."

CHAPTER 19

I HAVE THE ABSOLUTE WORST IDEA OF MY ENTIRE LIFE

"This must have to do with that Reckoning business the Hand was going on about," Dawkins said. And then, leaning into the wind, he walked toward the equipment.

"Shouldn't we be fleeing?" Greta shouted to him.

"Keep watch!" he shouted back. "I just want to see if I can throw a monkey wrench into whatever nefarious business they're planning up here."

"I'll help Jack," I told Greta.

"You sure?" she asked.

"Yeah. I've got this railing to hold on to." I pulled myself along the center until I reached Dawkins. By that time, he'd finished examining the bed frame thing and the lines connecting it to the metal rods and had begun going through the contents of four metal chests.

"Why all the emergency medical supplies? Not

just defib paddles, but . . ." He lifted up one vial after another and read each label. "Epinephrine—medical adrenaline, but also atropine, adenosine, and so on all the way down the alphabet—what are these for?"

He moved to the second chest. "Ugh," he said, slamming the lid shut. "Filled with weapons." He dragged it over to me. "We'll heave it into the East River before we head back down."

"Do we really have time for all this?" I asked.

"We must find out their purpose," Dawkins said. "You've met the rank and file in the Bend Sinister; most of them are morons. Which means that somewhere up here there are likely diagrams, instructions, *something* to aid the dimwits who put this together."

I glanced back at Greta. She raised her thumb and forefinger in an O: *Okay*.

"Of course, I could be wrong . . . Nope—here we are." From within the third chest he took out a folded sheaf of papers. He quickly scanned the first, flipped a page and scanned the second, then looked at the steel rods and rectangular frame in the center.

He stood abruptly, stuffed the papers into his coat, and frantically waved at Greta. "We have to get Greta away from here as quickly as possible."

"Why?" I asked. "What does this thing do?"

"I told you the thirty-six Pure are linked, right?"

"They each feel when one of them dies," I said.

"This"—he waved his hand at the entire setup—"this

is intended to transmit the death of a Pure to the other thirty-five, to use that single Pure soul as a window to reach and kill every last one of them."

"How . . . ?" I asked, backing away.

"These are lightning rods, Ronan, and those are transformers. The Bend Sinister will call forth thunderstorms, and guide the lightning—*all* the lightning—right here, straight to the Pure in that rack there. The Pure's heart will stop, and she will die, and her death will be carried via that bridge of stars I told you about to the other thirty-five."

"And they'll *all* die?" I asked.

"Maybe not at first," Dawkins said, kicking at one of the lightning rods. But it had been bolted to the stone, and he couldn't knock it loose. "But after the Pure dies, the Bend Sinister intend to revive her, so that they can kill her again, and again, and again—until the accumulated trauma kills the other thirty-five Pure."

"So all they've ever needed is one soul," I said. "That's why Dad risked burning down our house—he hoped my mom would somehow expose the Pure she was guarding." One hand on the railing, I reached down and grabbed the handle of the chest and started dragging it back toward Greta.

Dawkins hefted up the other end. "We are going to do everything we can to keep Greta safe. *Everything*. But if they capture Greta and discover the truth about her, we have to spare her."

"What do you mean?" I asked.

"We can't let them torture her like that. We can't let them kill her again and again."

"No," I said. "That would be awful. She's my best friend."

"More than that, we can't let them use her to get at all of the other Pures." Dawkins stopped walking and tugged the chest so that I had to turn toward him. He stared hard into my eyes. "Give me your word, Ronan: if they capture Greta, you will kill her before letting them attach her to this contraption."

"*Kill* Greta?" I glanced back at her over my shoulder. "There's no way I could—"

"Neither of us want her death, but we *cannot* let them do this. We *must* be true to who we are as Blood Guard."

The wind was fierce up there. My eyes were watering when I told him, "Okay. I promise. Now can we get out of here so that I don't *have* to do it?"

With his free hand, Dawkins waved to Greta and shouted, "Time for us to get off this landmark!" His voice sounded almost carefree, but I could see the strain in his face.

"What is that thing?" Greta asked as we drew near.

"Wasn't able to figure it out," Dawkins said. "Bend Sinister craft project, apparently."

"And in the box?"

"More of those Tesla guns," I said.

Dawkins and I set the chest down, and then he pushed it with his foot until it tipped over the edge. We didn't wait to hear the splash.

"Let's move!" Dawkins barked.

I couldn't look at Greta as she led us down the ladder on the other side of the tower, back to the suspension cable's other side.

She kept glancing at me, worried. "I'm really sorry, Ronan—but this part is going to be rough because of your fear of heights."

"I'll be okay," I said, shaking my head.

"At least we're going downhill," she said, squeezing my shoulder like my mom might do. "Hold tight to the auxiliary cables and keep your eyes on my back and we'll be at street level before you know it!"

"Fine, I'm ready," I mumbled.

Greta smiled and ducked down the ladder. And glancing at Dawkins, I turned and went after her.

Going down was a lot easier than going up, mostly because Krisco hadn't wrapped up much of this part of the bridge yet, and we could stand up instead of crouching in the tunnel of orange silk. But that was bad, too, because it meant I could see all too well exactly where I was—fighting the wind to walk down a steep, skinny cable, hundreds of feet in the air.

I kept my hands on the auxiliary cables and my eyes on my sneakers, and I didn't care about the Bend

Sinister agents who had probably figured out our escape and were even now climbing through that orange silk tunnel to the tower to search for us.

No, all I could think about is what I'd promised Dawkins I would do, and how I'd lied to him when I'd made that promise.

There was no way I could ever kill Greta. Not even to save her. I knew that, and at the same time I knew it made me weak, a failure as a Blood Guard, and a failure as her friend.

And, fine—maybe I cried a bit. My wet cheeks got cold in the wind, and I couldn't even wipe my face, because there was no way I was going to let go of those cables.

We were halfway down the main cable, and the slope had gotten easier as we got closer to the road. Another five minutes and we'd be safe.

Because I was watching the placement of my feet, I bumped into Greta when she stopped moving.

"Careful!" she said, as my right foot slipped sideways and I fell to one knee.

I felt Dawkins' fist grasp my collar. "I've got you, Ronan."

Greta looked back at my tear-stained face and said, "Oh, gosh, I'm sorry, Ronan—you must be terrified!"

"No!" I said. "I mean, yes, I . . ." I had no idea what to say.

"Why have we halted?" Dawkins said, stopping just behind me.

"The road," Greta said, ducking out of our way.

I didn't like what I saw: two figures climbing the cable toward us. Two men, one of whom I didn't need to see up close to recognize.

My dad.

"This is far too precarious a site for a sword fight," Dawkins said. "So I propose a new plan: we hurry back up and go down one of the cables on the far side of the—"

"That's not going to work, either," Greta said, nodding to our right.

Making their way up the other three suspension cables were the rest of my dad's team: one man on each of the center cables, and two others on the one farthest from us.

"Okay," Dawkins said, turning. "We go back down the way we came up, and at the cable's lowest point, before it enters the anchorage proper, we cut our way through the silk and climb down to the road."

"What if Legion and Birk and the Bend Sinister are coming up that way?" I asked.

"We will burn that bridge when we come to it," Dawkins said. "Now let's *go*."

Scaling the ladder to the roof of the tower was a cinch the second time around. I knew what to expect up there, knew I was in no danger of falling if I was careful.

The three of us crossed over to the other side and climbed back down to the main cable.

"I will reconnoiter," Dawkins said, brandishing his sword. "If we are to meet anyone on our way down, I'd rather *I* met them first. I am going to go *very fast* to clear the way. You and Greta follow as quickly and *safely* as possible. Ronan, you first, then Greta."

And then he spun and galloped down the cable, vanishing into the tunnel of orange silk.

"He wasn't even holding on," Greta said, tightening her grip on the auxiliary cables.

"It's easy to be fearless when you can't be killed." I bent over and led the way down.

"I'm right behind you, Ronan," Greta said, lightly tapping my back.

We had barely gone a dozen feet in the tunnel when I saw someone running full tilt toward us: Dawkins.

"Go back!" he shouted. "They're on their way!"

"But my dad!" I shouted at him.

"We'll take the cable on the far side of the tower," Dawkins said as he reached us. "I like my odds against two of his agents over the half-dozen Bend Sinister coming our way."

So for the third time that night, we headed back to the tower ladder. We cleared the silk-covered part, the loose ends flapping in the storm winds blowing around us, and I had an idea.

A terrifying idea. I thought I was going to be sick.

"What if there was another way off the bridge?" I asked.

"Out with it!" Dawkins snapped.

I drew my sword, went to the silk wrapping, and sawed through the side that went down to the roadway. One end of the fabric fluttered down toward the water, but the long piece that had been braided around it went slack. I grabbed the loose bit and started to hoist it up hand over hand. "This is all one big piece that's been wrapped around the bridge, right?" The fabric whirred over the auxiliary cable and puddled at our feet. "So what if we tie ourselves to it, and, um . . ." I couldn't stop myself; I turned and dry heaved.

"And jump!" Dawkins crowed. "That's idiotic—I love it! We might have enough silk to stretch all the way to the water. And the way this strand of fabric is braided around the others should slow our fall." Dawkins sheathed his sword and used both hands to help me. "We can just splash down and swim to shore."

"Like bungee jumping," Greta said. "Great idea, Ronan."

After a minute, we had filled the main cable between us. Dawkins tied Greta into the middle section.

"You'll be anchored here," he said, tapping her waist, "but to keep upright, you'll want to loop the excess around your leg here, and hook it across your back like so." He shuffled through another thirty feet

213

or so and then tied me in, and then another thirty feet to the end, and tied himself. "I'll be the dead weight at the end of the line," he said with a wink.

One by one, we climbed under the auxiliary cable and hung on facing out, our hands gripping the line behind us.

"Why are we always doing this?" I asked. "Jumping off things?"

"On three, I'll throw myself off," Dawkins said, ignoring me, "and you two do the same a split second after. Sound good?"

Sound good? No, it sounded *terrible*. But I swallowed and answered, "Okay," though I'd never been less ready for anything in my entire sorry life.

"*One*," Dawkins said.

"Let's *do* this!" Greta said. She actually sounded eager, like leaping to her death off the Brooklyn Bridge was something she'd been wanting to do forever.

"*Two*." Dawkins squatted and leaned far out, hanging on with a single hand.

"*Three!*" he shouted, and launched himself.

He leaped far, twenty feet out into the dark, trailing an orange silk streamer that I almost forgot was attached to me until the slack started to tighten.

"Ronan!" Greta shouted. "Go!"

So I squeezed my eyes shut and jumped.

CHAPTER 20

TAKING THE PLUNGE

B ack when I was maybe seven years old, I used to
like to hang my head out the car window when my
mom was driving. The rush of air on my face, the wind
blasting in my ears—it's what I thought it would be like
to soar through the sky.

"I'm like Superman!" I'd yell to my mom.

"No, you're like a dog!" she'd scold me. "Get your
head back into the car, Ronan, before something hits
it."

Falling from a really high place was a lot like that.
Windy, noisy, and somehow I knew that my mom would
not approve.

Maybe it wouldn't have been so bad if I'd listened
to Dawkins' instructions and held on to the silk. But
I hadn't, so I spun wildly as I fell, the world a jumble
around me. I opened my eyes and caught glimpses

of the half-wrapped bridge, the lights of the city, the dark, metallic crinkle of the waves on the river; heard the fabric snapping in the air, the faraway beeps and engine noises from the traffic, and someone screaming.

It was me, of course. Once I realized *that*, I shut my mouth.

Now and then I spotted Greta twirling above me, or flipped and saw Dawkins below, his arms and legs spread-eagled like a spider riding a strand of silk. At some point we fell past the roadway, the braided silk barely slowing us at all.

Would we hit the water before we ran out of fabric?

I've really *done it this time*, I thought. *I've finally done something* so stupid *that it's going to kill me, Greta, and everyone else in the world.*

And then the silk went taut and *twanged*.

As horrible as falling had been, jerking to a halt in midair was worse.

The silk Dawkins had tied around my waist yanked tight, but my arms and legs and head still wanted to keep going: I jackknifed around the knot and felt the silk cinch up around my middle. It felt like being cut in half.

Somewhere above, Greta moaned in pain. "Ugh!"

I looked up: she was maybe twenty feet under the bridge, the traffic speeding by above her. In the other direction, Dawkins spun in slow circles about eighty feet over the water. Me, I was stuck in the middle. We twisted in the wind.

"Not quite enough fabric, Ronan," Dawkins shouted.

I was in too much pain to respond.

"We're going to have to climb back up to the roadway!" he added.

Climbing a rope is easy . . . but silk isn't like rope—it's slippery. It was the middle of the night, we were all beyond exhausted, and when I looked down at the faraway water, I was scared out of my mind.

"Sure thing!" I said, and I started winding my fists into the fabric.

The silk jerked and rose a yard.

"Um, Jack?" I shouted. "Something's happening!"

I felt myself being dragged up another six feet.

"They're reeling us in like fish!" Dawkins shouted.

"Guys?" Greta called as the silk smoothly raised us all ten feet higher. "I can see the road—but I can't reach it!" The girders along the road were several feet out of reach.

"Swing!" Dawkins yelled, kicking his arms and legs like he was swimming through the air.

I tried swimming, too, but by the time our movements rippled up the fabric to Greta, we'd already been raised another twenty feet, and she was well past the roadway.

We rose smoothly and steadily after that.

"Cut me loose," Dawkins said.

"It's too far to fall."

"I'll be fine," Dawkins said. "Eventually. And then I'll bring help."

I drew my sword out and slashed at the fabric between us.

"And Ronan!" Dawkins shouted. "Your promise!"

My second swing at the silk cleaved straight through, and Dawkins fell, the silk whipping in the air behind him.

"Geronimo!" he shouted.

I lost sight of him under the bridge, but I heard a loud splash.

"Ronan!" Greta shouted. "Where's Jack?"

"Went to get help," I yelled, though that seemed like wishful thinking.

Only one person could stop the Bend Sinister now. And that person was me.

Too soon, I was being lifted up under the auxiliary cable by a team of five Bend Sinister agents, and then carried forward by three of them like a piece of furniture. They took me to the ladder, then handed me up to more agents who were waiting atop the tower.

I recognized Legion's team even before they rolled me over onto my face, tied my hands behind my back, and then set me on my feet next to Greta.

"Hey," Greta said, the wind blasting her hair all over her face.

"Hey," I said back. "You doing okay?"

She shrugged. "It's like four in the morning, a huge storm is rolling in, and we've been captured by a bunch of crazies up on the Brooklyn Bridge. So, yeah—I'm good, all things considered."

We were right beside the ladder, only a few feet from the tower edge. Bald pizza-eating man stood behind me, his hands on my shoulders; the dark-haired woman stood beside him, arms crossed, staring straight ahead. The redheaded agent had *her* hands on Greta's shoulders, while Legion's driver, a goateed gym rat with tattoos around his neck, was next to them.

Counting the four agents behind us, there were seven Bend Sinister members up on the tower. My dad and his team weren't among them. They should have reached the tower by now, I knew, so I figured they were lying low nearby.

"Let me do the talking, and if you get a chance, make a break for it."

"Forget it, Ronan," Greta said. "No way I'm leaving you behind."

The tall, white-haired woman in the red-and-gold robes walked toward us with her arms outstretched like someone welcoming you to her house. She was old, I realized—I mean, *really* old, like the sort of person who makes headlines when she dies because she'd been born before the wheel was invented or whatever. She was thin, but she didn't look frail. For some reason, I found her terrifying.

The old woman smiled at us. "So nice to meet you at last, Evelyn Truelove. I am Evangeline Birk." Like Dawkins, she had the faintest of accents.

"I've heard about you," I said. "You're even higher up in the Bend Sinister than my dad."

"Your father is *nothing*," Birk spat, the smile gone and her teeth bared. She shivered and the smile reappeared. "Though I must say, you bear quite the strong resemblance to him!"

"Lucky for me looks are only skin deep." I laughed like I'd said something funny. "Anyway, I take after my mom, not some Bend Sinister flunky."

Birk stared at me for a long time, the smile frozen on her face.

I realized what was so terrifying about her: She never blinked. Not once.

"He did lead us straight to you after years of hiding you from us," she said at last, "and for that, I am grateful." *Years of hiding you from us.* She thought *I* was a Pure. Why else would my dad have sacrificed so much to capture me? Why else would he have risked—and lost—the soul of another Pure, Flavia, at the Glass estate? And I suddenly realized only my dad knew the truth about Greta. He hadn't r evealed that to anyone.

"Good old Dad," I said. "I owe him a *lot*."

"Children bore me." Birk turned to Legion. "Prepare the equipment, and send word to the teams on shore. Everything must be ready by sunrise." She walked to the tower's edge and gazed out at the lights of Manhattan. "Our years of work are at last coming to fruition. The Reckoning is upon us!"

"What does that even mean?" I asked.

"It means a new day is dawning, Evelyn Truelove, one in which the old world will end and a new, better one, will rise up in its place. And you—you will have a front-row seat!"

"I'm curious about something," Greta said.

"Be quiet," I whispered. "Just let me talk."

Birk sneered at Greta. "What is it you'd like to know?"

"This whole end-of-the-world thing," Greta said, warming up like she used to do on the debate team. "It seems to me that the Bend Sinister is *part* of the world, so if you destroy the world, aren't you going to destroy yourselves, too?"

"No," Birk said. "An ark saved the blessed during the great flood, and now, when the great conflagration scours the earth clean, we will again take refuge in an ark."

"Sounds like a good plan," I said. "Listen. *I'm* the one my dad's been chasing, *I'm* the one he wanted to deliver to you. You've got me. Do whatever you have to do, but please, don't make my friend watch."

"How very touching," Birk said, raising an eyebrow. "Legion? Time for the examination."

"I'll bring it to you, ma'am," Legion said. She went and counted the metal chests, confused. "One of our lockers is missing."

"That was me." I shrugged. "It was full of guns, so I threw it into the river."

Birk leaned forward so that she could pinch my chin between her thumb and forefinger. "It won't be long now, Evelyn Truelove."

"Please, Ms. Birk, I prefer to be called Ronan."

Behind her, Legion reached into the fourth metal chest—the one Dawkins had never opened—and removed a black wooden case from within. She brought the box to her boss, falling to one knee in front of her and raising it up in her outstretched arms.

Evangeline Birk turned her back, and I wasn't able to see as she opened the case and took something from it.

When she faced us again, she held a shape-changing red mask I had seen only once before, worn by my father.

"*Le percepteur*," Evangeline Birk said, and I was able to place her accent at last. It was French. She was the same Madame Burque who'd killed Mathilde.

"Now, let's have a look at the two of you."

CHAPTER 21

THE RECKONING

I tensed, ready to throw myself at Evangeline Birk.

But that was an obviously dumb idea.

For one thing, my hands were bound behind my back, so I couldn't do much but head-butt her. For another, I had a Bend Sinister agent behind me with his hands on my shoulders, and a second agent standing next to *that* one, both of them armed. I'd never get anywhere *near* Birk, let alone stop her from putting on that mask.

So I leaped backward instead.

Bald pizza-eating man wasn't expecting that. He made an *oof* sound and his hands left my shoulders.

I bounced off him and fell to my knees, then rolled over and faced him.

He spun his arms in the air, trying to regain his balance as he slowly tipped back over the tower edge.

The dark-haired woman caught one of his hands, and the redheaded woman guarding Greta caught the other. He froze like that, leaning out over the abyss, his feet on the edge but his fellow agents holding him steady.

His eyes narrowed at me.

So I rocked back and kicked him square in the knees.

His feet shot from under him, and with a look of surprise on this face, he dropped out of sight.

Neither of his fellow agents let go of his hands, so the two women were silently yanked off the tower with him.

I didn't stop to congratulate myself. Instead, I got to my feet, turned, and charged straight at Evangeline Birk.

Some part of me was dimly aware of other things going on: Greta struggling to get away from Legion's goateed driver, stamping on his feet and shouting. And way on the other side of the tower, Legion's huge blond goon dropping whatever he'd been doing and pounding toward me.

But I was focused on Evangeline Birk. She dropped the Perceptor into its case and backed away at the same moment as Legion stepped in front of her, a sword drawn. "It will be a delight to cut you in two, Truelove!"

I ran straight for her. But when I was a few feet away, I dropped into a slide like Curtis Granderson stealing third, coming in under Legion's sword and far to her left.

"Missed us!" Legion crowed.

But I hadn't been aiming for them at all.

My right foot tagged the Perceptor case dead center. It skidded across the silk like a square hockey puck and arced out over the river, then plummeted toward the water.

Birk made a startled, furious noise.

"Sorry," I said. "I really hate that thing."

"I bet you do," Birk said. To Legion, she said, "Kill him."

"Gladly." The little dark-haired woman grinned and reared back with her sword.

Before she could chop down, I rolled away.

And came up against the dark leather shoes of the huge blond guy on Legion's team. He reached down, grabbed my shirt with one fist and my belt with the other, and lifted me over his head. I squirmed and kicked until he walked the ten feet to the side of the tower. I had a perfect view of the road a hundred feet below us. Even now, at four a.m., traffic was heavy down there. He bent his arms at the elbow, ready to hurl me.

"Stop!" Greta shouted.

"Yes, stop," Birk said. She sighed. "I've changed my mind. Don't kill him."

He paused and held me over his head like that, his arms quivering, probably debating whether to listen to his boss or to throw me anyway. Finally he sighed, spun around, and dropped me from chest height onto the rooftop near the ring of lightning rods. I stared at them and the silver metal frame in the center. I was probably going to be strapped to that thing soon.

I lay there for a moment trying to figure out what I could do next, when Birk and Legion walked over.

"I'll just send divers to locate the Perceptor," Birk said, tilting her head and shrugging. "It's practically indestructible."

"The Blood Guard will stop you," I said. "They'll be here any minute. They're probably swarming all over this place."

"We both know that's *probably* not true," Birk said. "But fear not: whether or not I have the Perceptor, the Reckoning *will* take place." She looked back and forth between me and Greta, deciding something. "Maybe you *are* valuable. Legion, have your man strap in the girl."

"Wait—what? Why?" I asked, sitting up.

"Slight change of plans, Evelyn Truelove. I'm going to test the device with the girl first."

The huge guy placed one of his big feet onto my chest and pushed me flat again.

"But she didn't do anything!" I said.

"Everyone is guilty of *some*thing, Evelyn," Birk said, chuckling.

Legion's goateed driver draped Greta over his shoulder.

"This way," the Hand said, and the two of them

walked a spiral pathway between the lightning rods around to the silver frame at the center, Greta kicking and shouting the entire time.

I squirmed a tiny bit and the giant leaned on his foot so that I could barely breathe. All I could do was watch.

There were leather cuffs at each of the four corners of the frame. Legion and the goateed agent used them to strap Greta in—a wrist or ankle at each corner.

"What are you doing?" Greta shouted. She was only twenty feet away, but the wind made it difficult to hear her. "What does this thing do? Ronan?"

And then Legion and the agent attached metal bands around her arms, legs, neck, and head. The bands, I figured, were connected to the transformers Dawkins had told me about, and those were connected to the sixty lightning rods.

"Nothing's going to happen, Greta!" I shouted. More quietly, to Evangeline Birk, I said, "Why do you want her to die? She hasn't done anything to you."

"But I *don't* want her to die," she said. "Instead, I want to kill her again, and again, and again, and for each of those almost-deaths to be carried around the world via the fiery bridge that unites all the Pure like her."

"But she's not a Pure," I said. "She's not."

"Then that will be evident, and she will have suffered for nothing." Birk wagged a finger at me. "But I suspect she *is* a Pure, and that's why you kicked my

Perceptor away. Because you, Evelyn Truelove, truly *are* a Blood Guard." She smiled. "I don't need *le percepteur* to see that."

"You're wrong," I said.

"Maybe! But if that's the case, then after we're done with her, it will be *your* turn."

Legion and the agent emerged from the lightning rod forest, and Birk said to her, "Have the Hands corral the storms and send them our way. We're ready."

• • •

Two more Bend Sinister agents climbed up to adjust dials and tweak settings on machines, and they chatted with Evangeline Birk while she pointed at this cord or that rod, and the whole time, I was trapped beneath the blond giant's foot.

He was enormous, a pro football linebacker in a pinstriped suit. He must have been six-foot-six and three hundred pounds—most of which seemed to be concentrated on my sternum.

No way would I ever be able to get out from under him.

The sky was getting brighter—the sun would be rising soon. Not that it would make a huge difference. Storm clouds were piled up to the horizon, their bellies dark and flashing with lightning. Any minute now, the Bend Sinister agents on the riverbanks would start directing that lightning here, with Greta its target.

She would be electrocuted.

The Bend Sinister would revive her.

And then it would happen all over again.

I'd promised Dawkins I would kill Greta rather than let her be tortured like this, but I couldn't even reach her.

I tried once more to get up, but the blond giant leaned forward even more. I wheezed and gasped until Greta shouted, "Stop it! You're killing him!"

Suddenly a jagged purple bolt of lightning crackled within inches of the blond guy's head.

"Get off my son!"

My dad was standing by the ladder from the suspension cable, a Tesla rifle in his hand.

The giant stepped away, and all at once I could breathe easy again.

Evangeline Birk opened her arms. "Why, Head Truelove, you have arrived just in time to join us for the Reckoning."

Another of my dad's agents appeared behind him, a bearded guy carrying a sword. At the same moment, the other four men in my dad's team climbed atop the roof from the other suspension cables. All of them were armed.

"Collect their weapons," Dad said, gesturing at Birk, Legion, and the three other Bend Sinister agents on the tower. The five silently took Legion's sword from her and collected two Tesla guns from the other Bend

Sinister agents. The older guy who'd sung lead on the subway patted down my big blond tormentor. But the goon wasn't armed. He didn't need to be.

"What is it you hope to accomplish here?" Birk asked. "Let's forget our differences and join in celebration of the change that is to come."

"That's not why I'm here," my dad said, strolling toward us across the orange silk.

I was still stuck on the ground with the blond giant looming over me. "No way are you here to save me and Greta."

"Of course not." He laughed.

Greta was too far away to hear our conversation. I couldn't imagine what she thought we were saying, or why my dad was acting like I'd cracked a joke.

"*Save* her?" He pretended to wipe his eyes. "No, I'm here to make sure she serves her purpose. She is a tool, a means to an end . . . once I've assumed command of this operation."

Evangeline Birk tilted her head. "Whatever do you mean, Head Truelove? I am, of course, grateful that you brought this Pure—whichever child it is—to our attention. Now why don't you have your team hand over their weapons. It's not too late for you to make amends."

"Oh, but it is too late for *you*," Dad said. He flicked a finger at her. "Four, please kill Ms. Birk."

The subway singer turned away from my blond

giant, leveled his saber, and slowly closed in on the white-haired old woman.

"No!" Birk said, backing against the central railing. "You don't have the loyalty of the teams on the shore below. They are waiting on word from *me*. Without me, they won't bring the lightning storms, and then nothing is going to happen here."

"Don't believe her," the subway singer said. "It's me they listen to, not her."

"What?" my dad said. "What's gotten into you, Four?"

It's Legion, I knew. *Legion had taken over my dad's team of agents.*

Behind me, the blond giant spoke. "Birk isn't in control here. It is Legion we follow now."

Beside my dad, his bearded agent said, "It is Legion we wait to hear from."

And then, at once, all of the Bend Sinister agents spoke in chorus. "Legion is the one who talks to the teams, so Legion is the only one who can lead."

Startled, my dad backed away from his own men. "Which one of you is Legion?"

"All of us," said every Bend Sinister agent on the bridge. They slowly closed ranks around my dad and Evangeline Birk, swords at the ready. Everyone seemed to have forgotten me and Greta. "To make way for Legion, we must kill Birk," said the tattooed goateed driver. "And Truelove, too."

"She's *there*, Truelove!" Birk shouted, pointing to where Legion stood still near the ladders to the cables. Her eyes were closed and she appeared to be almost in a trance. "*She's* the one you need to kill."

"Too late." Legion's eyes snapped open and she spoke into a cell phone. "Everything is ready up here. The order has been given. Time for the Reckoning!"

Almost immediately, the thunderclouds over our heads began to churn and the wind picked up.

Nearby, I knew, along the shores of Brooklyn and Manhattan, hundreds of teams of Bend Sinister agents were focusing all their powers on the skies, bending the weather to their will. This was why they'd been gathering since spring: to create the most monstrous lightning storm that New York City had ever seen, one that could lash the Brooklyn Bridge with bolt after bolt for hours.

And kill my best friend over and over again.

There had to be something I could do to spare Greta.

And suddenly I knew what it was—the very first thing Dawkins had warned me about, the secret he made me promise never to reveal.

"Greta!" I shouted. "It's *you*! *You're* the Pure!"

CHAPTER 22

THIS IS THE WAY THE WORLD ENDS

While I'd been lying there listening to my dad and Evangeline Birk bicker, I remembered something Dawkins had explained the very first time I'd met him, on the train from New York to DC: a Pure can't know *what* she is, or it changes *who* she is deep down where it matters. Self-knowledge ruins a Pure, and she loses that essential innocence forever.

Except hardly anyone even *knows* about the thirty-six Pure souls, so that kind of self-awareness isn't really much of a danger.

But there'd never been a Pure in the history of the world like Greta Sustermann. She was an annoying know-it-all who really *did* know it all. Unlike any Pure before her, she *knew* what a Pure was, and she understood exactly what it meant.

"*You're* the Pure! My mom and your dad—they were guarding *you*."

"You're joking!" Greta shouted, laughing nervously. "You have to be."

"She doesn't understand what you're saying, fool," Birk said. Then she saw my dad aim his Tesla gun at me. "*Does* she? How could she?"

"Don't make me kill you, Evelyn," my dad said.

The bearded agent under Legion's control snapped his arm up and yanked the Tesla gun out of my dad's hands.

"Oh my gosh," Greta was saying, looking at where she was: the frame, the forest of lightning rods, the Bend Sinister staring at her. "All of you are here because of me? That's silly . . . isn't it?"

"Someone has to stop him!" my dad shouted. "Evelyn, stop talking right now." He pointed at the huge blond guy. "You. Put your foot on his head." When the blond guy slowly moved his boot from my chest to my face, my dad turned to Legion. "Don't you get it? Stop my son from talking!"

"Greta, you *know* it's true!" I yelled. "Look inside your heart! And *hurry*."

Exasperated, my dad bellowed at Legion, "*What are you waiting for?* Have someone knock her unconscious! Have someone knock *him* unconscious! Throw him off the bridge! Do something, you idiot!"

"Kill them," Legion said.

"Finally!" my dad said. "Hurry, before it's too late."

"Birk and Truelove," Legion continued. "Take them out now."

"Do you understand *nothing*?" Dad yelled. He elbowed the bearded agent in the head, grabbed back his Tesla rifle, and broke into a run—straight into the circle of lightning rods.

"Come on, Greta," I whispered.

Greta's eyes were tightly shut, and she was muttering to herself.

"You're the reason my dad went after your mom! You're what changed Agatha! It's you! It's you! It's always been *you*!"

Listen to me, I thought. *You* know *what I'm telling you is true.*

"Oh my gosh. It makes sense." Her eyes widened. "It's *true*." She convulsed in her bindings before sagging, her head rolling forward.

"Greta!" I started to get up, then had to stop as the blond giant again pushed his boot against the side of my head.

My dad got to Greta as she slumped. He reached forward and put two fingers against her neck.

That was when it began.

A twisting fountain of white sparks shot up from Greta's limp body, hundreds of feet into the sky, like she was the world's biggest roman candle. A million swirling shards of light, a flurry of burning bright dots, a blazing river of stars silently poured out of her.

It was the most beautiful thing I have ever seen in my life.

And also the most horrible.

I blinked away tears and made myself keep watching. What had I done? Had I killed her?

"The stars!" Evangeline Birk cried. "We are too late!"

Far above us, the glimmering river of light split into thinner streams, like a tree's branches, and arced away into the night in dozens of directions. Thirty-five people around the world would feel a pang and not understand what it meant, but would feel the loss just the same.

The flow of stars tapered off into a trickle.

And then a pulse of energy exploded from Greta.

The light was so bright it hurt; if not for that big goon's shoe covering half my face, I would have been blinded. Half a heartbeat after the light was sound and wind and suddenly the huge blond guy's foot wasn't on me anymore because he was gone. I covered my ears, but it was already too late: all I could hear was a ringing that seemed to have swallowed the world.

After a few seconds, when I was sure it was over, I sat up and looked around.

Greta was still there, strapped into that rectangular frame, but we were alone on the silk-covered tower.

Everyone else had been blasted clear off the rooftop. Thanks to that giant's foot pinning me down, I'd been spared.

I shivered and stared at Greta.

A shimmery outline of light, made of the same bright sparks, slowly expanded from her. I could see Greta's shape in this outline at first, but not so much as it grew—bigger than the bridge tower, and after a while, bigger than even the bridge. The figure finally broke apart into a hundred thousand twinkles of light that seemed to fall upward and burn away.

She's made of stars, I thought.

When I stood up, I saw that I'd been wrong: Not *everyone* had been blasted off the rooftop. Evangeline Birk was lying on the ground, clinging to the central railing. Some of the other gear had also come to rest against the rail, and I went over and started rooting through one of the metal chests.

"What you did makes no difference," Birk croaked when she saw me. "I'm still going to kill her."

Greta wasn't dead? Startled, I hopped up, spun around twice, then crouched again to dig through the chest. "First things first," I said.

"What are you so happy about?" Birk snarled.

"Be quiet," I said. In the second chest, I found a utility knife.

"They are coming," Birk said. "You're not going to

escape this place, you know. But if you help me, you can depend on my pity."

I extended the blade. "I *asked* you to be quiet," I said.

She closed her mouth as I walked away.

Weirdly enough, most of the lightning rods were still standing. The shock wave hadn't affected them. Was that because they were so thin?

Greta hung limp in the metal frame, held up by her arms. She looked dead. I unclasped the metal bands from her arms, legs, and head, then kneeled and used the knife to saw through the leather bindings around her ankles. Finally, I cut away the bands at her wrists.

She fell forward into my arms, and, man, was she heavy. I had to ease her to the ground because I couldn't figure out a way to carry her. I pressed my fingers to her throat and felt a pulse. She really *was* alive.

I needed to get her some help. I looked up, and that was when I saw it. There was a clear path through the lightning rods, a straight line to the edge of the tower where they'd all been knocked out of place.

My dad. It had been his body that mowed down the lightning rods; the shock wave had blown him this direction. I followed the destruction, through the thicket of rods, all the way to the northern edge of the tower roof.

When I got close, I found something surprising: two hands clinging to a twisted bolt of the orange silk.

I got down on my hands and knees and crawled to where I could peer over the edge and see him.

"Ronan!" he gasped, and laughed.

It was the first time he'd called me Ronan since . . . since I couldn't remember. A long time.

"Boy, am I happy to see you. Help me up, will you?"

I started to stretch my hand out, but something told me that was a bad idea. "Hold on while I find a rope."

I scooched back, then got up and looked around. Most of the Bend Sinister's junk was gone now, and there was no rope anywhere to be seen. But there *was* a lot of electrical cable connected to the lightning rods.

Within a few minutes, I had what I needed. I tied one end of the cable to the center railing, made a loop in the other end, and made my way back to my dad.

"Put that loop around your shoulders," I said. "You'll be more secure. In case you slip."

"I am not going to slip, Evelyn," he said, releasing his right hand and quickly winding the cable around his forearm.

While he was doing that, I said, "You know that Damascene 'Scope thing?"

"Yes, Evelyn, of course I am aware of the Damascene 'Scope."

"It *works*," I said. "It really works." I felt something new about my dad, something I hadn't felt about him in ages. Hope, maybe. "It can burn the bad right out of a person. I've seen it happen! It changed this woman

Agatha Glass from evil to good. It could work for you, too. You could go back to how you used to be—a good man."

"Evelyn," my dad said, wrapping his other arm in the cable and hoisting himself up a foot. "There is no bad in me to burn away." He pulled himself up another foot. "I do what I do because it is the right thing to do."

"Dad," I said, stepping out of reach, "what you do is *wrong*."

"I can tell you this with all honesty, son: I have done nothing I am ashamed of."

"But you were going to kill Greta," I said.

You were going to kill me.

If I'd been a real Blood Guard, I suppose I would have kicked him in the face and sent him plummeting to his death. Or used my knife to cut the cable he was using to pull himself up. Or done anything to stop him from climbing to safety.

Because he was a bad guy, and I knew it—had known it, for a very long time.

But he was also my dad, and there were some acts I realized I'd never be able to carry out. So I just sat down and watched him muscle himself back to safety.

He had half his body up and was trying to swing up a leg when footsteps behind me made him look up.

"Not the welcoming party I'd hoped for," he said. He suddenly sounded tired.

I turned, and there behind me were my friends, my

240

family—my mom, staring lasers at me, probably out of her mind with worry; Mr. Sustermann, who'd already broken away to run to Greta; Ogabe, bigger even than the blond giant who'd kept me under his foot; Diz, her sunglasses on and her pile of pink hair a windblown mess; and Dawkins, still damp, but wearing a crazy big smile like the one he'd worn when I first met him.

"What took you so long?" I said.

"I went for a swim." He laughed. "I figured you had everything under control."

Then Dawkins stretched out his arm to my father and said, "Mr. Truelove, let me give you a hand."

"No, thank you," my dad said. He caught my eye. "Good-bye, son."

And releasing the cable, he fell backward out of sight.

CHAPTER 23

THE NEW WORLD

Back in eighth grade social science, I had to write a paper on this scientist named Harlow who did a lot of experiments with baby rhesus monkeys. I got a B+, which was completely unfair, but that's another story.

Anyway, his work was all about figuring out how babies bond with their moms. Or, in the case of this one twisted experiment, with a cloth-covered wire armature that the baby *thought* was its mom, but that randomly shot out spikes every now and then, hurting the little monkey.

But no matter how often the baby monkeys got hurt by their wire robot mamas, they always came back. Because, this Harlow guy figured, they longed for a mama, needed a mama, and that spiky wire robot mama was the only one they had.

It broke my heart, reading about those experiments.

And it broke my heart when my dad fell off the bridge.

That's the only way I can explain why I cried out, "No!" and slammed my fists into the silky orange tower rooftop and crawled forward until my head was hanging over the edge. I imagined that if he looked up, he'd see me watching him fall, just like he watched me in my dream.

None of this changed what I knew in my heart: My dad was an awful man. A bad man. The worst man, maybe. I knew all that. But I cried anyway.

It took me a while before I realized that my mom was there with her arm around me, holding me back. Maybe she thought I was going to jump after him.

"I'm okay, Mom," I said. "Really."

"Good, because I'm not," she said, her voice gravelly. "I'm sorry, Ronan. No son should have to see his dad . . ."

"Is he like those other Bend Sinister agents?" I asked. "Will he come back to life?"

"Afraid not, kiddo," she said. "At least, not as we understand things. We could always ask that white-haired crone back there."

She was pointing at Evangeline Birk, who'd not only been bound hand and foot, but also gagged.

"I wouldn't trust her to tell the truth," I said.

My mom laughed, but it sounded so fake that we both raised an eyebrow. And then she laughed for real.

"Used to be, you cut down one of the Heads, and seven more would appear in his place. But this Birk woman is higher than the Heads." My mom pressed her forehead against mine. "She's the real heart of the Bend Sinister. We lock her up, and they will be in disarray for a generation at least."

"Won't the rest of them come looking for her?" I asked.

"Who knows? But if they do, we'll be ready."

"She's the monster who created the Perceptor," Dawkins said, walking over. "But I'm guessing you figured that out, Ronan."

I nodded. "And about the Perceptor—I kind of kicked it off the bridge. It's somewhere down there in the water."

Dawkins' smile was the biggest I'd ever seen from him. "Are you pulling my leg?" he asked. "It's *gone*?"

And then, before I could stop him, he grabbed me up by my armpits and raised me high like a baby, shouting, "Well done, Evelyn Ronan Truelove! Well done, indeed!"

"Put me down!" I said. "You're going to make me sick!"

"I happen to know you've eaten nothing since you last vomited some nine hours ago. Ergo, I am safe."

He set me down anyway.

"I've longed for the destruction of that thing since I was seventeen," he said.

"Birk says it's indestructible," I said.

"I'm willing to accept that challenge," Dawkins said. "I'll find that monstrosity and see just how indestructible it really is."

"Am I happy to see you," I told him.

"Ronan," he said, clapping my shoulder, "I have never in my life been happier than I was on seeing you and Greta alive and well." At the startled look on my face, he said, "Okay, Greta is not in the *best* of shape, of course—she's been through the proverbial wringer—but she's *alive*, and so are the other thirty-five Pures, and, well, it is all thanks to you."

I leaned in and whispered, "I broke my promise, about . . . Greta. I—I blabbed that she was a Pure. I told her!"

"And it was a *brilliant* move, Ronan. And one that had never occurred to me, because until Greta joined our ranks, it was virtually impossible. No Pure has ever been 'woken up,' so to speak, because no Pure has ever understood what it meant to *be* a Pure." He hugged me tight. "You saved her, Ronan. Thank you."

"How'd you even get here?" I asked, breaking away. "When I cut the silk, you—"

"Fell a long way," he said. "From that height, striking the water is like slamming into concrete; I, um, broke many bones—more, I think, than I actually have in my body. Felt like that, anyway."

"I'm sorry."

"Don't be. It was necessary," he said. "And lucky for me, our friends saw a body go into the drink trailing a big orange silk tail."

"Somehow I knew it would be Jack," said Ogabe. "Call it intuition, if you wish, though it probably had more to do with his hollering 'Geronimo!' as he fell."

"Nothing else was appropriate."

"How did you know to come to the bridge?" I asked Ogabe. "That Hand took our phones away."

"Yes, but not before Sammy located your signal and figured out your direction," Ogabe said.

"Everything pointed to the bridge," Sammy said, appearing behind Ogabe. "The way the Cat-o-Grapher site told us the cat was in the river near the bridge; the direction the van that took you guys was going. It was a lucky guess."

"So we mobilized three-dozen retired Guard to help us search the anchorages at either end," Ogabe said. "You, of course, know what we found."

I laughed. "I *warned* Birk that you guys were probably already here, and she didn't believe me."

"What's unbelievable," Sammy said, "is that we're standing on the *top* of the Brooklyn Bridge!" We both looked out. The clouds had broken and sunlight was poking through, making New York look about as pretty as it ever gets.

"Unbelievable is one word for it," I said.

Then the six of us—me, Dawkins, my mom, Ogabe,

Sammy, and Diz—gathered around Greta and her dad.

There were dark circles under Greta's eyes, and she was having trouble keeping them open, but she was awake and looked like herself. What I mean is, she looked supremely irritated.

"So I'm a *Pure*?" she said to me and Sammy. "Seriously, you guys?"

"Technically, not anymore," Dawkins said. "You need the past tense: *was*."

"How could you not *tell* me? You're my best friends."

"Greta, you know perfectly well why they couldn't tell you," her dad said.

"That whole Pures-can't-know-what-they-are rule—I know!" Greta said. "But Ronan, if I found out something like that, you'd be the *first* person I'd go to with the secret."

"That makes no sense, honey," Mr. Sustermann said.

"No, it makes perfect sense," I said. "You're right, Greta. I'm sorry."

Greta nodded. "I forgive you. And thanks for stopping whatever it is they were going to do. What were they going to do, anyway?"

Dawkins fluttered his hand at her. "Oh, a typical bit of Bend Sinister tomfoolery. Why dwell on it? Instead, let's get off this windy pile of bricks and find ourselves some breakfast."

"I could eat my way through some pancakes," Sammy said. "And eggs. And I wouldn't say no to bacon."

"Samuel," Dawkins said, "you're singing my tune."

"Food would be nice," Greta mumbled. "And sleep, too. But didn't Ronan's big mouth just set into motion the end of the world as we know it?"

"Thanks a lot!" I said.

"I've got to call 'em like I see 'em," Greta said.

Ogabe said, "It's true: Ronan *did* just dispel the soul of one of the thirty-six Pure, so once again, the world *is* off-kilter."

"Terrific," I said, and put my head in my hands. "Because of me, the world is messed up again."

"But it's not so simple as all that," Ogabe finished.

"Why not?" my mom asked.

"Because this has never happened before," Ogabe said. "No one has ever 'woken up' a Pure before."

"So does this mean I don't have a soul anymore?" Greta asked.

"You still have your soul, Greta," Ogabe explained. "But the overlay of purity you'd carried is no longer part of you. Before, your example and mere presence subconsciously influenced those around you to be better people. And now . . ." He flipped his hands up and shrugged.

"Now *what*?" Greta asked.

"You're just a regular person."

"That's okay with me," Greta said. "I'd rather be a regular person, if I had to choose."

"So what happened to her Pure soul?" I asked.

"That is the great mystery!" Ogabe said. "How does a Pure soul behave when it has been woken up like this? Does it wait for reincarnation, like the souls of Pures who have been murdered before their time? Or is it immediately reborn back into the world as part of another person?"

"I guess there's no easy way to find out," I said.

"On the contrary," Ogabe said, "the Grand Architect can gather a quorum of the Blood Guard, and that group can project the Spangled Globe. It reveals the locations of the thirty-six Pure."

"You guys mention this architect person a lot—who is she?" I asked.

"Used to be a she," Diz said, looking at Ogabe, "but the title was passed on, and now it's a *he*."

"While you four were taking part in the Glass Gauntlet," Ogabe said, "I was helping the Grand Architect of the Guard pass out of this life. She gave her responsibilities to me—along with the history of the Guard, a knowledge of its lore, and an ability to pinpoint Pure souls wherever they may be around the world."

"That's this Spangled Globe thing you mentioned?" Greta asked. "So when are you going to do that?"

"Tonight," Ogabe said. "Thanks to the events that have transpired here in New York City, we have as large a grouping of Blood Guard as has been together since the 1970s—more than enough people to project a clear vision of the Globe."

"So maybe I didn't doom the world after all," I said. "I got lucky."

"Come *on*." Sammy rolled his eyes. "We *all* got lucky. We did this together."

"Sure," Greta agreed. "Lucky us."

CHAPTER 24
THE SPANGLED GLOBE

That night, the Blood Guard gathered in Madison Square Garden.

"Let me guess," I asked Dawkins, "a retired Blood Guard works as a janitor here."

"Don't be absurd," Dawkins said, using a flashlight to light our way down the steep concrete stairs toward the floor.

"So maybe a retired Blood Guard owns the place?" Sammy suggested, his head pivoting around nonstop. "It's big!"

"I only *wish* we had members with such resources," Dawkins said. "No, we chose this site because there are no events tonight and we needed a large, private space."

"Then how'd we get in?" I asked.

"Let's just say that no doors can withstand the Sustermann father-daughter lockpicking team."

Descending the stairs in front of us were Agatha, Greta, and her parents. Her mom still seemed a little stunned by everything Mr. Sustermann had told her, but they'd come here together, and when I looked at them, they were holding hands.

I'd been to the arena only once before, to see a basketball game with my dad, and the building had been brightly lit and filled with people. This time, we'd left the lights off, and there were only about forty of us.

I knew six of the Blood Guard—Dawkins, my mom, Mr. Sustermann, Ogabe, Diz, and the old lady from Wilson Peak whom everyone called the McDermott— but the rest looked like they'd just wandered in from the street. There was an Asian man in a chef's apron, a nun, a construction worker, two firemen, a woman who looked like a fashion model, and an old lady who looked like a grandma. There were three women in business suits, and just as many guys in those full-body coveralls like the custodians wear at school. And there were others, more than I could take in. A few of the Guard seemed to know each other, but mostly they just stood alone, waiting for Ogabe to tell them what to do.

Dawkins steered us to a row of seats where Agatha and Greta's mom were already sitting. "Normally, this is a very secret procedure," he said, "but you lot know so much already that there's no point keeping you in the dark." He turned his flashlight off. "So to speak."

"What's going to happen?" Sammy asked as Dawkins flipped it back on.

"The forty of us will stand in a big circle, and we will raise our Verity Glasses to our foreheads," Dawkins said, tapping his index finger against his skull.

"The sigil!" I said. Each of the Blood Guard, I knew, bore a mark on his or her forehead invisible to the naked eye, a tiny knot of eternal flames that curled up and wound around each other. It was only through a Verity Glass that the sigil could be seen.

"Exactly," Dawkins said. "The sigil flame not only marks a Guard's purity of purpose. It also functions as a light source—one that can project an image through the Verity Glass."

"Of this Spangled Globe thing?" Greta asked. "So why do you need all these people?"

"Because the projection from a single sigil isn't sharp enough for the Grand Architect to read. Each Guard possesses the entire image, but in a blurry, out-of-focus form. It is only when enough are projected together that the image gains clarity. As you will see."

It sounded a lot like how the Bend Sinister's Perceptor worked, combining the "pure sight" of many people to make the Pures of the world visible. But unlike the Perceptor, no one was going to have to sacrifice anything to create the Spangled Globe, I thought, remembering those empty bodies Dawkins and Mathilde had found in the glassworks.

Ogabe called out to him. "We're almost ready, Jack."

"Excellent! If you all will excuse me," he said, then went and joined the group. They looked very small and far away in the dark of the arena.

"You're free to do whatever you want now, Greta," I said, looking past her at her mom and Agatha. "You can ditch the Blood Guard and just go back to your old life."

She frowned. "What makes you think I want to go back to my old life? What if *this* is what I want to do?"

"But you're not a Pure anymore," Sammy said. "You don't have to worry about the Bend Sinister coming after you."

"Sammy, I didn't join the Blood Guard because I was a Pure. I did it because I admired the people in it, and because I believed they do good in the world. I still believe that."

"And now that you're not a Pure," I said, "it'll make it a lot easier for all of us. For starters, we won't have to keep lying to you."

"Or let you win things just because you're special," Sammy added.

"That's a lie," Greta said. "You guys never *let* me win anything. Don't try to make excuses now. And don't call me *special*."

"Okay, okay," I said, "you win. We won't talk about how special you are."

She slugged me, but I just laughed, so she slugged me again.

"Guys," Sammy said, pointing. "They're starting."

The forty Blood Guard held hands and formed a big circle with Ogabe in the center. The whole time they were doing this, he was speaking, chanting, working through some sort of incantation. And then one by one, the Guard raised their Verity Glasses to their foreheads where the sigil invisibly burned.

And in the air over Ogabe's head, a sphere woven of violet light appeared. It was sixty feet across, fuzzy, and dim. But as each new Guard raised his or her Verity Glass, it grew brighter and clearer.

"It's the earth," Sammy whispered.

When the number of Guard projecting the image topped twenty, the continents were clearly visible; after twenty-five, we could make out the raggedy edges of coastlines, the dark dots of island chains; when all of the Blood Guard had joined in the projection, it was like looking at the planet from space.

And then Ogabe added his own Verity Glass to the projection, and the flames began to appear.

They were small—like the flame from Dawkins' Zippo, only burning white-hot—and brighter than the globe itself. And I couldn't be sure, but if I had to guess, I'd say there were thirty-five.

Using his free hand, Ogabe reached up into the air and began turning the sphere, throwing his fingers wide and making it bigger so that he could zoom in on each tiny flame.

I think he was identifying each of them.

He paused and looked out at me.

"Ronan," he said. "Come join us."

"Me?" I said, reaching up and touching my Verity Glass where it once again hung from a chain under my shirt. "But I'm not a Blood Guard." *Was I?*

"And yet you bear the sigil," Ogabe said.

I reached up and touched my head, like I'd be able to feel it.

"Something must have changed up there on that bridge," Ogabe said, "because the sign is there that you are one of us. And right now, we could really use your help."

"Get up there, Ronan," Sammy said.

"Don't worry," Greta said. "We'll still be here when you're done."

As I walked up to the ring of Blood Guard, it widened, creating a space between my mom on one side and Dawkins on the other.

"Stop dawdling," Dawkins said. "If I hold this pose much longer, I'm going to get a crick in my neck."

My mom reached out with one hand and squeezed my arm.

I copied them, resting my Verity Glass against my forehead and staring up at the glowing sphere of light above us.

And maybe it was the addition of my lens, or maybe it was just chance, but right at that moment, a new flame flared into existence somewhere in the Pacific Ocean.

"There!" Dawkins said, pointing.

"Wow," I breathed, watching the tiny flower of white light twist and curl upon itself. I glanced over at Sammy sitting next to Greta, but they were staring over my head, at the Spangled Globe. I felt proud of myself for the first time in a long while. Greta was still here, and so was I, and the spinning world above me was still in balance.

It doesn't get much better than this, I thought.

Ogabe turned the globe in his hands, zoomed in, and considered the flame. He looked down at me and smiled, then beamed at all of us. "Ladies and gentlemen, we have a new Pure. Welcome to the world, little one!"

ACKNOWLEDGMENTS

For details about Monsieur Vidocq and Paris of the mid-nineteenth century, I am indebted to Graham Robb's superb history of the city, *The Parisians*. Just about every story in his book is more fantastical than the one I concocted in *The Blazing Bridge*. Better yet, the stories are *real*.

All the folks mentioned here have been enormously kind and generous during the creation of this novel, and listing them seems a paltry way of expressing my gratitude. Nonetheless, my heartfelt thanks to:

The Fluffy Pink Unicorn Preservation Society: Nicholas Tedesco, Will Hoffman, Jean-Luc Tessier, Yael Fishman, Hannah Ott, and Sophia Kalandros.

Dennelle Catlett, Deborah Bass, Timony Korbar, Tanya Ross-Hughes, and Katrina Damkoehler at Amazon/Two Lions helped this book and the two before it shine both literally (by giving the books lovely jackets) and figuratively (by promoting the novels to readers everywhere).

Thanks to Vivienne To's stunning artwork, this book and the previous two are beautiful to look at and to hold. The Blood Guard are very lucky that she lent her talents to the series.

Editor in chief Kelsey Skea. She always makes time for her authors, and is, it turns out, one of the two lions the imprint is named after.

Editor Melanie Kroupa must certainly be the other one, because there is no other way to explain her bottomless patience and lionlike dedication to this book and series.

Robin Benjamin stepped in at the last minute to carry the book over the finish line, and I am beyond grateful for her kind attention and help.

Genevieve Herr, Emily Lamm, Stephanie Thwaites, and Sam Smith of Scholastic UK are exactly the sort of international allies one dreams of having watch your back. (Genevieve especially is good in a knife fight.)

Ted Malawer is a giddy wit, sounding board, and idea generator, and also a friend. His help, as well as that of Dan Bennett and Bruce Coville, has been, as usual, invaluable.

Beth Ziemacki and Georgiana D., for everything, always.

CARTER ROY worked some three-dozen jobs ranging from movie theater projectionist to delivery truck driver before finally ending up as an editor for a major publisher, where he edited hundreds of books before leaving to write. The author of *The Blood Guard* and *The Glass Gauntlet*, he is also an award-winning short-story writer. He lives in New York City and can be found at www.carterroybooks.com.